A RARE OBSESSION

ALSO BY SHELDON RUSSELL

A Forgotten Evil

A Particular Madness

Listen

A RARE OBSESSION

SHELDON RUSSELL

cennan
chester county,
pennsylvania

PUBLISHED BY CENNAN BOOKS
an imprint of Cynren Press

Chester County, Pennsylvania
http://www.cynren.com/

Cynren is a registered trademark of Reodgyfen Inc.

Copyright 2025 by Sheldon Russell

Thank you for buying an authorized edition of this book, which will ensure that the author is compensated for his intellectual property. All rights are reserved. Thank you for complying with copyright law by not reproducing, storing in a retrieval system, utilizing for purposes of training artificial intelligence technologies, or transmitting, in any form or by any means, electronic, mechanical, photocopying, recording, or otherwise, any part of this book in any form without the prior written permission of the publisher.

No generative AI has been used in writing or producing this book.

First published 2025

Printed in the United States of America

ISBN-13: 978-1-947976-58-0 (hbk)
ISBN-13: 978-1-947976-59-7 (pbk)
ISBN-13: 978-1-947976-60-3 (ebk)
ISBN-13: 978-1-947976-74-0 (lgpr)

Library of Congress Control Number: 2024951320

This book is a work of fiction. Any references to historical events, real people, or real places are used fictitiously. Other names, characters, places, and events are products of the author's imagination, and any resemblance to actual events or places or persons, living or dead, is entirely coincidental.

Cover design by Roderick Brydon
Typeset in Arial 16 pt

In Memory of Timothy R. Russell

Chapter 1

Unable to turn over on the narrow couch, Ethan struggled to reach the blanket that had slipped to his knees. He shivered against the frigid air that fluttered the window shade and whispered from the darkness. Locked under his body, his arm zinged from lack of oxygen, but he slept on, trapped at the edge of consciousness, his eyes squeezed against the morning dawn.

Once, he thought he heard her call out his name. Turning his ear into the silence, he listened again, and then again, for her to reassure him that together they could make things right. But there was no apology, not this time. This time had been harsh, cold, and irreparable. This time the words exchanged had shattered about them, painful, shards of broken glass.

He first heard Olivia's name in a college classroom, Classical Greek History, and the perfect place to encounter a goddess. From that moment, he was struck with her beauty, with her blue eyes, her translucent, marble skin. Once he had spotted her sitting in the back, the chiseled profile and sensuous mouth, he could think of nothing else. By the end of class, he had not the faintest idea of the lecture, nor had he taken a single note. What he did know with certainty was that he had fallen in love.

***

From the first, he had made it his life's goal to know her, to sweep her away with every action and every word in his cache. And he thought the while that she was beyond reach, but they found one another, without caution and in unguarded places. They took each other where and when they could, in a moment, in a fury, to strip away clothes and bask in the scent and heat of lovemaking, and then to hear her husky voice and feel her nails on his flesh. Nothing else mattered, save the next time, because in that, their very lives existed.

Their love was fierce and intense, shared only by a deepening curiosity of all things literary and bookish. They were swept up in the promise and excitement of discovery, feeding on each other's needs and dreams, failing to see the collapse of their relationship. They talked endlessly of philosophy and dissected the most esoteric and remote theories. Their debates at times were heated, competitive, out of control, and their love for each other began to fracture.

They graduated together, a perfect moment as they received their diplomas, and with the good wishes of all who had supported them, even though, as he was to learn later, their friends had doubted from the beginning the durability of the relationship.

The strangest of all was his own denial. He'd first seen them from a distance, their hands clutched over the table. But he'd failed to confront her. To acknowledge the deception was too devasting, and so his denial postponed the finality of it all. He knew, of course, that it couldn't be sustained, but it was all he could do. He had no choice.

***

He turned on his side and willed himself asleep, awakening now and then in the shallowness of his dreams. And when she entered the room, he knew that she was there, standing over him.

Opening his eyes, he stared into the dark truth that she had spoken only hours before, that it was over, that there was someone else, that she no longer wanted to be with him. And with a turn of her shoulder, she'd banned him to the couch to await the morning's departure.

And then he saw her there in the hate and blackness, her arms lifted above her, the blade glinting in the moonlight. He struggled against the softness of the couch, his blanket knotted about his legs. He waited for the fire and sting of the blade, the suffocation and dread it would bring as his lungs filled with blood.

"Olivia, don't," he said, choking back the fear that paralyzed him.

The shadow hesitated, then turned. The front door swung open. He could smell the night, moist and fresh, and he could see the curve of her back as she walked away. Her hair lifted about her face in the night breeze, and she was gone.

Chapter 2

She'd left without paying her share of the rent. Without that, he could no longer afford the apartment, which in some ways was just as well. Everywhere he looked were memories of their time together, the bottle of Chardonnay left over from their graduation celebration, just the two of them late at night, the stack of thrift books they'd read and discussed endlessly, clothes she'd left behind—the scent of her birthday perfume.

He searched for a job—or, not *searched* so much as *worried* about a job. He'd managed to spend four years of his life and thousands of dollars pursuing a degree that now struck him as worthless. He was drowning in student loans. His car was ready for hospice, and his heart was irreparably broken.

So, he searched for work by walking aimlessly about, past the library, past the city lake, through the park. He searched for work by replaying that moment that she'd stood over him, knife in hand, with the intent to take his life. At least that's what he'd thought. As the days passed, he was less certain. It had been a dream, or his own damaged ego at play. It was, he supposed, beyond knowing at this point. But what *was* certain was that she was gone. He was alone, and his future had turned empty.

Reality further hit home when the notice arrived to either pay the rent, vacate the apartment, or risk an eviction lawsuit. It was destiny, pure coincidence, that a check from his father arrived that very same week. His father, emotionally wounded from the death of his second wife, had cut off Ethan's funds and disappeared from his life. The money was reparations.

It was a modest amount to be sure, but it *was* a check, and the first break he'd had. So, with money in hand, he set out to find a place to live. But it was soon apparent that the amount was even less valuable than he'd thought. Not only could he not find a place to rent, no matter how humble, but he would still be faced with utility costs, deposits, and a dozen other things.

He'd found the camper for sale in the want ads and at a good price, but small, tiny actually, and with little more than a bed, a two-burner stove, and a shower, one so cramped that he could barely reach his feet. He'd paid cash for it. The remainder was used to pay the first month's parking fee, and a deposit to cover the possibility that he might pull out in the middle of the night unannounced.

And so he moved in, discovering that his world had shrunk to such small dimensions that there was no room for the books he had so carefully collected over the years. So it was with sadness that he loaded them into the car and abandoned them in the alley behind the thrift store.

The following weeks served only to feed his gloom. To save gas, he parked his old car and walked instead. The few job interviews he managed to arrange were doomed from the outset. It was, no doubt, his depression, adolescent to be sure, but real and visible to everyone. Who wanted to work with some heartbroken dope?

To make matters worse, he'd spotted them together again, and face-to-face this time as they exited a downtown coffee shop. He'd opened the door and confronted them, their arms locked. He stepped back to let them pass, and her eyes caught his briefly. But she did not acknowledge him. He'd imagined a different encounter, but it had vanished in that single, icy moment.

That chance meeting spiraled him downward into the depths, wiping out what little progress he'd made. He struggled to sleep, waking in the darkness, replaying what had happened over and over, a mantra of depression and rejection. He ate little, and badly, grabbing from his tiny fridge anything that didn't require preparation. His ambition waned, and the curiosity he'd so carefully nourished over the course of his education faded. His walks were aimless and wandering and failed to revive him. More than once he'd sat alone on a park swing and considered final options.

The job opportunity came to him unexpectedly, a chance meeting with an old acquaintance from college, someone who had witnessed the drama firsthand. It was temporary and not the job he'd wanted, not the dream—not even close—but it *was* a job.

Chapter 3

He walked through the tunnel that ran under Main Street and connected the Administration Building with the high school building proper. The air was stale and smelled of the heat and intensity of youth. He could have eaten at the cafeteria and spent his lunch hour talking to his fellow faculty members, but this was the last day of the semester and, more importantly, the last day of his job.

The teaching position had been offered with the understanding that the previous teacher would be returning the following semester, after having successfully delivered her baby. The classroom he'd been assigned, a small room on the second floor of the Administration Building, had isolated him from the faculty at large.

The pay had been adequate, given that Middleton was a refinery town flush with tax money and high-salaried corporate types. While such riches provided luxuries unusual in that part of the country, the ever-present smell of methane was a constant reminder of its source.

Busy as he was—adjusting to teaching, dealing with adolescents and their parents, sitting through the ever-dreaded faculty meetings—the semester had passed quickly. Despite its difficulties, it had been worth the effort. It had kept his mind off himself and required him instead to think of others. The end result was that the semester was suddenly behind him, and he was faced once again with unemployment—the crucial difference being that he'd managed to make considerable headway in the meantime. While he'd not forgotten her betrayal, he was much more able to keep the pain at a safe distance. It was time he moved forward, and that was exactly what he intended to do.

Directly below his classroom was the plush office of the superintendent of schools, complete with a conference room, richly furnished with leather chairs and a mahogany table the size of an aircraft carrier. His own classroom, on the other hand, had not seen paint in forty years. The windows rattled against the never-ending winds, and the furnace intake had been known to suck students' homework right from their desks.

He'd never really entertained the notion of teaching before, taking the job out of pure necessity, but it had brought him face-to-face with his own struggles. Like most people, he had experienced all the angst and loneliness of the age, made the same mistakes, and had the disquieting suspicion that he was somehow unacceptable to others. Now, after watching it play out in his students over the weeks, he had come to a personal revelation and a more accurate sense of who he was.

That was not to say that the job wasn't difficult, that it didn't require an enormous amount of energy. And, of course, there was the whole business of dragging all the conflicts and troubles home with him, leaving him stressed and anxious about what course of action to take. These conflicts stayed with him far too long, sometimes even into the thin hours of dawn. At the beginning he was emotionally drained by the weight of it all. Now, looking back, he could say with confidence that those weeks and those students had taught him as much as he had taught them. But although he would miss them, he was more than ready for solitude and peace.

Standing at the window of his classroom, he looked down onto the street. From there he could see the city's Carnegie Library, a beautiful old building within walking distance of the school. Oil and corporate influence had funneled substantial resources into stocking its shelves and building a world-class collection of rare books. Being able to see the collection had been an interest of his for months.

He'd often stood in that very spot, drawn by the mystery and ostentation of the library, wishing he'd had the opportunity to browse the collection, though it had been the consensus of his colleagues that, though the collection was enormously valuable, it was highly secured and rarely used. Few were permitted access to its hallowed shelves. Now, as he gazed on the library, he couldn't help but mourn his own small collection that he'd abandoned in the alley on that sad day.

As a child, he'd often found refuge in the quiet world of his hometown library, a small, one-room structure, an unassuming building donated to the city upon the death of its owner. It was managed by a single librarian, a woman of age whose name he'd never learned. He'd been drawn to her quiet, gentle way. She'd treated him as a person, a friend, someone worthy of being in her sanctuary.

His shyness had waned in her presence and under her guidance. Her warmth and love of books had grounded him in the unpredictable world of adolescence. And what he'd discovered on the shelves of that humble little building had been a source of high adventure and excitement that had remained with him his whole life.

Even his closest friends had not known how complicated his life, how eccentric his ways, and he'd protected those secrets at all costs. But as the years passed, he had been increasingly drawn to those pursuits. He'd looked for that passion in others, especially her, and was convinced that he'd found it. What he'd found instead was a keen intellect, an analytical and practical mind, rather than a passion. What *he'd* wanted was spiritual, not intellectual, a hunger fed through curiosity and the need to explore and to know. He'd wanted someone to share that with him because he found peace there and an odd sense of comfort. Both she and he had been mistaken in each other's desires, and the cost had been high.

He sat back down at his desk and opened his gradebook. When he had completed his reports, he signed and dated them and took the classroom key down to the secretary, who was just leaving for the day.

"It's after five," she said. "Couldn't this wait until tomorrow?"

"Sorry," he said. "This is my last day."

She took his records, dropped them in her desk drawer, and asked that he sign in his key and enter the date. From there he left the school for the final time. There would be the usual flurry of angry telephone calls from parents. Disappointed and tearful students would drop by to protest their grades. But this time would be different. This time he would be gone.

Chapter 4

Spring stirred in the afternoon breeze as Ethan walked through the park. The children's play area had been constructed not far from the lake, complete with its swings, a merry-go-round, and a couple of picnic tables. A woman sat at one of the tables, watching a boy at the swing set. She wore a headscarf and a coat too warm for the weather.

The boy studied his feet and twisted back and forth as he grasped the chain above his head. Ethan knew neither the woman nor the child, not in any authentic way, but he sensed their isolation. There was the absence of joy that can happen in such an empty moment. It was missing in the boy's movements, the way he hung his head, failing to sense the world around him. Ethan wished for him friends, and play, and conversation, all required for happiness, but then caregiving was no longer his job. The world was full of waifs and lost souls, none of whom was any longer his concern. There was misery enough without setting out to find more. This was his time now, time to be free, no more grades, no more schoolyard, hall duty, or lonely, angry kids.

His personal life had been neglected under the stress of teaching. All else and all others had taken precedence over himself. His sense of self-worth had been neglected under the constant diligence of the job. Now he could regain all that. Now he could enjoy who *he* was and what *he* loved once again.

Of course, there was the small matter of money, or more specifically the lack thereof. He had groceries, for a while at least, and a place to sleep, so he was better off than some. What he wasn't certain of, even at this point, was what he wanted to do with his life. With luck, maybe he could find out.

He walked on through the park and to the lake with its dilapidated pier. He made his way out a ways and paused for a moment to listen to the soft slosh of waves as they pushed onto the shore. A faint smell of fish hung in the air, and in the distance, a boat hummed across the lake. He'd never been a fisherman, but he could appreciate its allure. There was something healing and serene about the water.

He thought about her and what she might be doing. Were they married, or living together? Did they make frenzied love in the middle of the night? Had her lover watched from the couch as she walked away to another man, or had she stood over him with knife poised? He hoped so. He hoped they were both filled with loathing and misery.

He walked on toward home and had gone but a short distance when something moved in the grass that had grown tall in the dampness of the backwash. His heart ticked up, and a chill raced down his back. Like in any city park, there was always the possibility of being mugged. He paused to listen, and the rustle came again. And then he saw it, a small dog, the identical color of the dried grass in which it hid.

Two black eyes looked out at him from the grass. Always a sucker for animals, he squatted down and waited. This one was scared, hungry, dumped into the park, the kind of cowardly act he despised.

"Come here, boy," he said, holding out his hands. "It's OK. I won't hurt you."

The dog moved forward a little, sticking its head out from the grass. He could see its tail fanning at high speed, its delicate legs pumping with anxiety. Ethan moved forward, beckoning the creature with his fingers, but the dog turned and disappeared once again into the tall grass.

***

The camper rocked under his feet when he stepped in. He'd not taken the time to secure it properly when he'd moved, and it now pitched under his feet like a boat at sea. He fixed himself a scotch and turned on the radio. He closed his eyes and tried to relax. He could still feel the banter and stir of the classroom. How long would it take to free himself from the drama of the adolescent world?

Something then stirred him out of his stupor, a sound, a voice maybe. He turned his ear and listened again. Neighbors came and went daily in the RV park. It was something he was going to have to adjust to. And when the sound came again, he recognized it as a dog barking. He opened the door and stepped out. Across the drive was the little dog he'd seen at the lake, a male, a mutt, maybe part Chihuahua. He was wet and covered in mud. When Ethan started toward him, he ran away.

Ethan lay down in his bed and thought

about what might lie ahead. He thought about the boy, the one on the swing who'd studied his feet as if answers might materialize there in the sand. That was he, Ethan Poser, a little older now perhaps, but still in search of something.

Chapter 5

Ethan rose early the next morning determined to find work. He fixed breakfast, then sat at the kitchen table to make a list of what he considered to be his strengths.

After that, he searched the newspaper in an effort to match current job listings to the strengths he'd listed for himself. First identified was Hanson's Storm Door & Window Sales, which had posted a public relations position.

After finishing his coffee, he read over the listings again, refining each into specific skill sets. He was well read. That was good. It wasn't every one who had read the complete works of William Shakespeare or who could quote from memory the prologue to Chaucer's *Canterbury Tales,* and in Middle English at that. He'd authored lots of research papers, too, and anyone who had ever encountered a professor could certainly appreciate that.

And as for the public relations part, he'd been dealing with kids and their parents day in and day out for a semester—public relations at its best. Throw in faculty meetings and pandering to the ever-omniscient administrator and you had public relations on steroids.

The dog was nowhere in sight when Ethan set out for Hanson's Storm Door & Window Sales. It turned out to be a prefabricated building near to the lumber yard. He'd passed it often without ever really noticing that it was there. He checked his tie, took a deep breath, and went in.

Windows and doors were prominently displayed in the showroom, each touting superior insulation ratings, double-pane windows, and expert installation at reasonable prices. A middle-aged man sat on a stool behind the counter. His glasses were thick, and his brows swept upward above them like miniature ocean waves.

"May I help you?" he asked, setting aside his paper.

"My name is Ethan Poser," Ethan said, clearing his throat. "I'm here about the public relations position."

"Bert Hanson," he said, reaching out his hand. "I'm the owner. My office is in back."

Ethan followed him, his stomach tightening

at the prospect of an interview. He waited for the owner to close the door.

"Sit there," Hanson said, pulling his chair up to his desk. "Now, you are applying for the PR position, is that correct?"

"Yes," said Ethan. "The public relations."

"You strike me as being young for such a position, Mr. Poser. What is your experience?"

"Well, I have an English degree, and I've been substitute teaching."

Mr. Hanson looked over his glasses again. "You've been teaching public relations?"

"No, sir. English, high school English."

"And what makes you think you are qualified for a public relations position, Mr. Poser?"

"Teaching is all about that, isn't it? I mean, building relationships is a critical part of teaching. I've read widely. I'm a communicator."

"And what do you think you would be communicating here?"

"Well, the quality of the product, its value, like that."

Hanson opened his desk drawer and pulled out a brochure, pushing it over to Ethan. "Everything you ever wanted to know about doors and windows is in that brochure. And, frankly, a hell of a lot you don't want to know."

He closed the drawer. "Mr. Poser, anyone who comes through that door to purchase windows and doors is convinced of one thing. You know what that is?"

"No, sir."

"That they're going to get screwed."

"Screwed?"

"That's right. They've heard all the stories about rushed jobs and cheap products. The only others on the block with less public trust than window and door salespeople are used car salespeople."

"I see."

"So a public relations man has one job here, and that's to change the perception of that customer, to convince him that he's going to get a first-rate job, with a smile, and that it's going to save him a fortune in heating costs. In other words, that he isn't going to get screwed." He clasped his hands in front of him. "Now, do you think that teaching high school kids qualifies you to perform that work successfully?"

Ethan sat for a moment before sliding back in his chair. "No, sir," he said, "probably not." He walked to the door and paused. "It isn't true, is it?"

"What isn't true?"

"That they're going to get screwed?"

Hanson drummed his fingers on the table before answering. "Why do you think we need a PR man, Mr. Poser?"

Chapter 6

By week's end, Ethan had interviewed for a technical writer's position with Stout's Power Tools, which turned out to be writing instruction manuals for their air compressor line. The co-owner, a man who kept him waiting for over an hour, failed to see Ethan's teaching experience as appropriate for the air compressor business, or anything else for that matter.

Ethan's final stop a week later was a listing for a web designer. Even he could see how useless he would be in the position. His visual creativity did not extend beyond fourth-grade cartoon drawings, and his knowledge of computers was not much better.

The short of it was that he found himself woefully unprepared for a world that moved too fast and in ways that left him cold and disinterested. He was extinct, killed by his own hand—and by his archaic interests. He'd been born too late for the modern world.

Saturday came with no job and no

prospects of finding one. He slept until eight—not slept so much as lay in bed—rejected and unwilling to face the day.

Afterward, he drank a pot of coffee while staring out the window of his camper. Job hunting on a weekend was not a clever idea. His money was getting painfully low, and he dared not recklessly spend what was left. He had no friends, beyond the few he'd met while teaching, and he had no desire to resurrect the past at this point. Ethan read the paper one more time before deciding that he could not bear another day waiting in the camper.

***

He found the lake calm and the park absent of people when he got there. He took a moment to walk to the end of the pier to enjoy the morning. The breeze was moist off the lake, and a flock of birds lifted and fell on the gentle waves in the distance. But the need to find work soon robbed him of the peace he sought, and he walked on toward town.

As he approached, he could see the terra-cotta tiled roof of the library rising above the trees. It was a beautiful building, constructed with the best of everything, built of riches, and he'd always wanted time to explore it. He would get a library card. Last he'd checked, they were free, as were their benefits. And what better way to spend the weekend?

He stood in front of the imposing structure and looked up at its facade. It was a grand building, a Carnegie Beaux-Arts with all the beauty and extravagance there in its form. The front steps were wide and high, like open arms, and a lamp located near the bottom step lit the entrance at night. The front doors were strong and noble, so big and heavy that he struggled to open them against the morning breeze.

Inside, bookshelves stretched toward the ceiling, and the air smelled of books and leather. The ceilings spiraled upward, secured with dark and massive woodwork, carved and oiled like cathedrals of old. Objets d'art poised silently about the grand gallery, a bust of Andrew Carnegie, a little boy with a book open on his lap. Great, sweeping paintings hung in any available space, purchased at any price with the library's plush resources. Above, doors encircled the mezzanine and led into shadowed and secret places. A dazzling Victorian chandelier glowed high in the reaches of the rotunda.

Ethan approached the front desk, where a young lady with copper hair and olive skin leafed through a file drawer.

She looked back at him over her shoulder. "May I help you?"

Ethan's pulse took an extra beat at her emerald eyes. "I would like to get a library card."

She closed the file drawer. "Are you a resident?"

"Yes."

She handed him a form. "Fill this out, please. We will need a permanent address."

He sat down at a table, filled out the form, and took it back to her.

She looked it over and said, "This is an RV park address, sir. I'm afraid we will need something more permanent."

"It is permanent. I mean, I live there."

"But it's an RV park, isn't it?"

"Well, I'm looking for a house, you see, but in the meantime . . ."

"I don't know," she said. "We have a very strict return policy."

"I taught at the school just up the street. I was an English teacher."

"But you are no longer there?"

He shook his head. "Temporary. The regular teacher returned from leave."

"Let me check on this, Mr. Poser. I'll only be a moment."

He waited at the checkout station as she made her way back to the office. A sign over the door read DR. BATES MORRIGAN, LIBRARY DIRECTOR, and another handwritten sign in the office window read "Job Opportunity. Apply Within." A man with dark-framed glasses sat at the desk. He took the application and read it, glancing over the librarian's shoulder at Ethan.

When she returned, she handed him a library card and smiled. "Dr. Morrigan said we could make an exception. Do let us know if your address changes, Mr. Poser."

"Yes," he said. "Yes, I will. Thank you."

She smiled, and the light from the chandelier caught the copper tint in her hair.

"Was there something else I could help you with?" she asked.

"Ah, well, I was wondering where the fiction section might be?"

"It's upstairs. Would you like for me to show you?"

"Would you, please?"

He followed her through the stacks and to

the stairs that spiraled upward to the mezzanine. He could smell her perfume, vanilla, and he could hear the swish of her nylons against her skirt as they climbed the steps.

When they reached the landing, she paused, looking back at him. "Are you still with us, Mr. Poser?"

"It's grand," he said, pointing to the chandelier.

She looked up. "I love it every day. Now, the fiction section begins here. Were you looking for anything in particular?"

Not wanting to reveal his taste for mystery, he hesitated. "Ah, how about Hemingway? There's nothing to compare to the great American novel, I always say."

"Then we have something in common. I've read the entire collection of American novelists, and it's quite extensive, as you can see." She trailed her finger along the row of books. "Hemingway starts here. Do you have a specific title in mind?"

"I'll be back when I have more time to browse," he said.

She pushed her hair back, which had drifted over an eye. "My name is Anna. Feel free to ask for me if you need additional help."

"I do have a question."

"Yes?"

"That door there, the one that says 'No Entry Without Permission.'"

"That's the library's Special Collections room. It's rare books and documents. The collection is one of the finest in the country. Quite valuable, actually."

"Rare books," he said, looking at the door. "I've heard about the collection."

"It's quite extensive. Dr. Morrigan, our director, is a well-known scholar and archivist. We are lucky to be supported by a generous foundation as well. The end result is an archive that enjoys national recognition, not only for the collection's rarity but for its contribution to research. Special Collections has professional preservation and restoration functions as well."

"Old books are like time machines," he said. "All those voices from the past."

"Well, yes, I suppose that's true. They do command a certain reverence. I've noticed it many times with patrons who are permitted access to the books."

He walked over to the door, which was heavily secured with a bolt lock. "Are they available to be seen? I mean, might I look at them?"

"Oh, I'm afraid not, Mr. Poser. Dr. Morrigan is extremely strict about who has access. They are much too valuable for general public use. Millions of dollars have been invested in them, you see, and most cannot be replaced at any price. Qualified researchers can make arrangements, of course, but Dr. Morrigan is cautious about exposing the materials to just anyone. Care must be exercised in their use. I'm sure you understand?"

"Oh, yes," he said. "I do understand." He followed Anna back down the stairs to the checkout desk. "Thanks for your help," he said. "It's a beautiful library."

"Do come back and see us," she said. "And if you need assistance, there's always someone to help."

"And so you work here full-time?" he asked.

Anna smiled. "Anything else I can do for you, Mr. Poser?"

"One last question."

"Yes?"

"About the job opportunity?"

"Job opportunity?"

"The sign in the office window back there. Is it for a librarian's position?"

"Oh, that. No, we are in need of a custodian."

"Oh, I see."
"Are you interested?"
"No, no, thank you. That wouldn't be for me."

Chapter 7

He sat on the edge of his bed and ran his fingers through his hair. He knew, of course, that finding work soon was critical, that it was more than time to get on with it. He'd had rough spots before in his life, like the time his high school girlfriend dumped him with a note written on the back of a hall pass. He'd survived all those dark moments, and he was determined to get through this as well.

It was just a matter of attitude, of getting back up and going for it, of looking forward to the possibilities instead of looking back at the failures. He searched out his stash of mini composition books and put one in his pocket. Why he carried them, he didn't exactly know— to bolster the illusion that he was organized and had the world under control?

So, with his resolve fortified, he spent the morning researching job listings once again and recording them in his notebook. He took a shower, shaved, and used his special cologne.

So, today was the day. Today he'd secure a job one way or another.

***

The first stop was a small business office that had advertised for someone to create blog material. It turned out to be a freelance kind of thing, writing promo narratives for other people. The subject matter, and one's expertise in it, didn't seem to matter. As ill-informed as he was about the digital world, he understood that writing blogs for other people about subjects he didn't know or care about might not make the best career.

He reviewed his notebook and checked other possibilities: a part-time grant writer at the Department of Agriculture on Fifth Street and St. Catherine's and a listing for a medical writer at the local hospital, to start immediately and with benefits.

First up was the guy at the Ag Department, who looked him over and said, "It's writing grants, government grants, for everything from pesticide controls to landowner demographics. Grants are the lifeblood of the Ag Department. Without grants, we wouldn't exist. What qualifies you for the position?"

"I was an English teacher," Ethan said.

"A what?"

"Teacher."

"The federal government wants everything spelled out in a formalized way, Mr. Poser. If you need a million dollars, you write the grant for two million. Do you see what I'm saying? That way they can give you a million and still be happy because they screwed you for a million."

Ethan looked at his hands. "I can learn," he said. "I'm good at learning."

"It can't be learned," he said. "It's a special kind of character flaw that only a few are blessed with."

Ethan shook his head. "I don't understand."

"Have you ever run for political office, Mr. Poser? Ever been arrested for fraud or tax evasion?"

"No."

"Ever failed to pay child support?"

"Not ever."

"Exactly, and that's why this position isn't for you. Good luck in your search."

Ethan sat in his car and took deep breaths. OK, he wasn't going to work for the Agriculture Department, so he'd try the hospital.

He passed through the revolving door of

St. Mary's and approached the checkout desk, a mammoth structure, big enough to keep sick people at a safe distance. The reception area smelled of rubbing alcohol, and an elevator down the hallway dinged continually.

He was directed to see a woman at the Personnel Office. Her hair was the color of orange marmalade, and she wore earrings that stretched her lobes to her jaw line.

"Medical writing requires a thorough mastery of medical vocabulary, Mr. Poser."

"I'm good with words."

"And it requires the ability to decipher doctors' handwriting."

"I've graded research papers on Edgar Allan Poe written by eighth-grade boys."

"But you've never broken the Enigma Code?"

"Well . . ."

"And there are challenges in the medical field that require strong defensive assets."

"Dealing with death? I can do that."

"No, subjugating your opinion and pride to every man who ever graduated medical school."

"Well, I don't think that is required, is it?"

She pulled an earring off and rubbed her

lobe. "Spend a day at the nurses' station and then talk to me again, Mr. Poser."

***

Running low on funds, Ethan stopped by the bank to check on his account. He was a week away from an overdraft, and the parking space fee at the RV park was coming due.

The next two days he spent alone in the camper struggling to figure out his next move. He reread his notes and considered different scenarios. It was on the third day, after a cold breakfast of cereal and half-soured milk, that he made up his mind.

He shaved, put on his Levi's, sneakers, and a denim shirt, and headed out through the park toward town. The woman and the boy were at the swing set when he went by, but neither acknowledged him. The little dog he'd seen earlier was sunning at the end of the pier. He passed the school where he'd taught, now quiet and dark for summer vacation. The morning sun reflected from the windows of his old classroom on the second floor of the Administration Building.

The library was just opening when he

arrived. The copper-haired girl had been replaced by a young man, who explained that he was the Saturday help and that Anna would be back on the job Monday.

"I was wondering about that sign back there in the office window," Ethan said.

"The custodial job?"

"Yes, that one."

"What about it?"

"Do you have an application? I'd like to apply."

Chapter 8

Anna Khole parked in the street outside her bungalow. Not having a garage was one of the things she missed the most about living downtown. But it was close to the library and freed her from a long commute. On really nice days, she could even walk to the library, taking a shortcut through the park.

She'd lived in the house for a year now and had grown accustomed to the noise that accompanied city living. Being a librarian was not exactly everyone's dream job, she supposed, but it had been what she'd wanted her whole life. It came from both happy days and sad days that she'd spent in the library when growing up. It came from a child's imagination unleashed.

She'd found the career of a librarian pleasant. Working among the books was strangely rewarding. She was safe among the spirits of storytellers and prophets. She sensed their gratitude for her attention and care. At least, that's how she thought about it. Working there was like spending her days with old and wise friends.

Of course, the job wasn't all that all the time. There *was* the public to deal with on a daily basis, and not everyone had lofty ideas about books and knowledge. There were those who saw the library as a place of security, a refuge from dangers at home or the traps of the street. Others saw it as a place of warmth when the snow came and the winter winds blew. Of course, there were those few who saw it as a place of temptation, exploitation, and propaganda, those who sought to censor and control it. But all who came through those doors believed in one way or another that they had a legitimate right to be there, no matter the reason.

Academics had been her forte, an area of her life where she'd felt in control. Of course, being a nerd had not always served her well in high school. Weekend parties and prom dates had not been something she'd sought out. She'd found most boys overly excited and immature. Not that she considered herself better, only different. College had brought with it an older crowd, of course, but little in the way of emotional maturity. She now dealt with a diverse and sometimes challenging public.

She fixed herself an iced tea and turned on Mozart's overture from *The Marriage of Figaro.* She thought about the guy who had gotten a library card last week. Something about his demeanor interested her. She'd seen how he'd walked the gallery, studied the art, demonstrated enthusiasm for the rare book collection. Most people dismissed the archives as simply a depository of old books and of little relevance to their own lives. Most had no sense of the contributions to scholarly research those books represented or even of their monetary value, which could easily reach into the millions of dollars.

The fact that their library had amassed such a remarkable collection had to do primarily with Dr. Morrigan's reputation as an archivist and the fact that the city was the center of the largest oil refineries in the country. The book collection contributions were favored tax write-offs for many of the town's wealthy. Although Dr. Morrigan was not an easy boss, there was no denying his influence when it came to the library's reputation.

When the phone rang, Anna's pulse

picked up. She knew what day was coming but had not allowed herself to think about it. It would be her mother calling.

"Hello," she said.

"Anna, this is your mother."

"Hello, Mother. How are you?"

"You do remember whose birthday it would have been tomorrow, Anna?"

"Danny's birthday," she said. "I hadn't forgotten."

"I just want to make sure he's remembered."

"I'll take some flowers in the morning."

"So many are forgotten, you know."

"I'll call you later."

"Yes, and let me know. Goodbye, dear."

"Goodbye, Mother."

***

Anna had set her alarm for five o'clock and rose in the darkness. She retrieved the empty jam jar that she kept in the pantry for such purposes. Dawn was just breaking as she picked the lilac blossoms and put them into the jar.

The drive across town to Riverside Cemetery took less than thirty minutes through the vacant streets. She placed the flowers on the grave and stood in silence as the morning broke. The scent of the lilacs graced the morning air. Her eyes welled with tears.

Danny had been born late into the family, too late for the normal adjustments in relationships to occur. Her mother, in her later years by then, had been shocked by her unplanned pregnancy. Even Anna's father, deeply involved in his career, was unprepared for Danny's arrival. Anna herself, a young teenager struggling with identity issues, found herself on the outside. The end result was a family drifting apart.

That was when Anna had turned to books for emotional support. By entering into that world, she was able to defend against the sudden loss of her place in the family hierarchy. It was those lonely years lost in her books that spawned a lifelong interest in literature.

Danny, too, more than any of them, had struggled with his untimely arrival. Early on, he sensed that he was responsible. By then their mother struggled with the challenges of menopause and physical decline. Their father was increasingly irrelevant, both in the family and at work, and Anna entered young adulthood, that critical point when one's course in life must be firmly established.

Danny sensed the isolation and resentment the most. He sought acceptance anywhere it was to be had, and it was most available from Anna. She struggled to give him what he needed, but it came with deep resentment. Sometimes, in unguarded moments, her feelings exploded, and she said things that she should not have said, which only increased his need for affection.

He searched her out in embarrassing moments, when her friends were there, if a boy showed her the slightest attention. At the heart of it all was Danny's need for what was rightly his. Ironically, his death might have saved them all, if only Anna herself hadn't killed him.

Chapter 9

Ethan sat at the table in the RV drumming his fingers as he read over the form for the custodial job. It was a boilerplate application with the usual questions about previous employment, recommendations, and education. He filled it in, emphasizing his experience as a soda jerk in high school, where he had been required to keep the place clean.

This job *was* custodial, after all. They needed someone to sweep the floors, clean the bathrooms, and stay out of the way. He could do that and take his salary until something better came along. Maybe it was just the sort of thing that would be best for him right now. He had a lot of thinking to do about his life and where he was headed. Maybe this job would give him just the time he needed to do that.

***

The copper-haired girl was at checkout when he got to the library.

"But this is for the custodial position, Mr. Poser," she said.

"It *is* still open?"

"Why, yes, I think it is, but . . . I mean, I had the impression you were an educator, a teacher."

"A temporary teacher," he said. "Listen, Miss . . ."

"Anna," she said. "Anna Khole."

"Listen, Anna, I really need the work, and I'm up to doing the job."

Anna looked back at the office, then at the application. "He's in—Dr. Morrigan, I mean. Would you want to see him now, or we could make an appointment if you prefer?"

"Now would be fine."

"You may wait over there. I'll check."

He sat at a table and took a careful look around, this time with the eye of a person who might be cleaning the place every day. It was larger somehow, filled with heavy furniture, shelves, and study carrels. It would be quite a task for one man to keep up. For a brief moment, he considered leaving. Surely there was a better way to survive.

"Dr. Morrigan will see you now," Anna said, returning.

"Thanks," Ethan said.

Dr. Morrigan was grizzled and lean sitting behind his oak desk. A scar showed through his thinning hair. His eyes were large, but then his glasses were thick, giving him a permanent surprised expression.

He looked over Ethan's application and leaned back in his chair. "This is a six-day-a-week job, Mr. Poser, and the library is a busy place. It must be kept clean for the public at all times."

"Yes, sir," Ethan said. "I understand, and I would be available to work six days a week."

Morrigan slipped off his glasses and rubbed his eyes. "You do know that your experience for this job is rather limited, and you've no specific recommendations here?"

"I'm new in town. I filled in a semester teaching at the high school. They are out for the summer, but I'm sure they would be glad to talk to you. I thought it prudent to apply while the position was still available."

He laid his glasses on the desk in front of him. "This is a public institution. People come in here for all kinds of things. They might be doing important scholarly research or just looking up grandpa's genetic credentials. You never know. But all of them expect to be left alone by the staff, to have quiet, privacy, and confidentiality. That would include you. You'd be expected to do your work and not involve yourself in anyone else's business."

Ethan nodded. "I understand. The job would be to clean the facility and to not interfere."

"Exactly," he said, checking his watch. "Now the board has given me leeway to fill this position without a vote. Assuming you were offered the job, how soon could you begin?"

"Immediately," he said. "Today."

"We would not have you starting today, Mr. Poser, but the job has to be filled soon. You'd be responsible for maintaining all floors of the library. The Special Collections room on the mezzanine level houses some of the rarest books in the world. It is not open to anyone without my permission, and that would include you. The books are irreplaceable, and they must be secured at all times."

"I understand."

He lifted his pen and clicked it with his thumb. "I'm prepared to give you a try, Mr. Poser. If your work is acceptable, we can make the position permanent. I expect you to be here early every day to open the library and late to close it at the end of the day. There is a utility room downstairs for your things and a storage area for supplies. You can start Monday, if you find these terms agreeable."

"Monday works fine," he said. "Thank you, Dr. Morrigan."

"Take this application back out to Anna. She will fill out the necessary papers, provide you keys, and conduct a walk-through. When you arrive, always come through the back door. Shut off the security alarm by entering the appropriate sequence of numbers. Anna will provide those to you. The front doors are equipped with a tag security system that sets off an alarm if a book has not been scanned properly. Have the doors unlocked and the lights on by eight. Any questions?"

"No, sir."

"Fine," he said, turning in his chair. "And no smoking on the premises."

Ethan found Anna shelving books in the biography section. He handed her the application. "I'm hired," he said, smiling.

"Congratulations," she said, offering her hand. "Now, understand that I am the associate librarian here, which means most of the detail work lands on my desk. Dr. Morrigan is the director."

"Dr. Morrigan said you would conduct a walk-through."

"And when do you start work?"

"Monday morning."

"I have most of the information I need here on the application to complete the paperwork. Would you care to do the walk-through today? I do have some free time."

"Yes, please. That way I can get myself organized for Monday."

They started in the basement utility room where his shop was located, a small and dark room with a high, narrow window at ground level. There was a large closet, a chair, a desk, and an old, two-drawer file cabinet. The room smelled slightly of mold from the damp and lack of sunlight.

"The cleaning supplies are in here," she said, opening the door to the closet. "And that door back there leads to the old furnace room, which is no longer functional. We have bathrooms on all floors that have to be cleaned daily. Make sure there are paper towels and toilet paper at all times. These are public bathrooms, you understand. Sweep all floors daily, mop weekly, empty trash each day and in all offices, clean the front doors, because kids have no idea how to open a door without both hands placed firmly on the glass. Occasionally we do have an emergency that might require your assistance."

"Emergency?"

"The boys like to plug the stools from time to time, just for the excitement, I presume, and the girls write obscenities on the mirrors with their lipstick. Smoking, and that includes weed, is forbidden. Any such transgressions should be reported to me or Dr. Morrigan, preferably me, not only for your sake but for mine as well. Breaking the rules has a way of ruining Dr. Morrigan's day, which in turn ruins mine.

"One other thing—if, while performing your custodial work, you see a patron deeply engaged in their research, it's best not to disturb them. Having quiet and privacy is a priority here."

"Got it," he said. "I taught high school. You'd be surprised at the nature and number of emergencies I've dealt with."

"You are welcome to eat your lunch in your shop. That's up to you. Don't have friends in during work hours. Dr. Morrigan doesn't like it."

"Right," he said.

They climbed the stairs to the mezzanine area. "As I told you before, that over there is the Special Collections room. It's Dr. Morrigan's pride and joy. Many of the books in there are quite valuable, one of a kind, and require exceptional care and attention. Access is restricted, and the rules are strictly enforced. You will have no responsibilities in the Special Collections room.

"As you know, Dr. Morrigan is an archivist of some repute and keeps a close eye on the collection. It's largely his reputation, along with the foundation's resources, that has made this library guardian of one of the most extensive and unique collections in the country."

"Has Dr. Morrigan been here long?"

"Many years, and most of them as the director."

"Have you seen the collection—personally, I mean?"

"Yes, I've assisted Dr. Morrigan on a few occasions when we've had important writers and scholars visit the collection. But Dr. Morrigan himself conducts all acquisitions, including trades, cash transactions, and estates. You see, much of what we acquire comes from private collectors. Dr. Morrigan's negotiations must work within the confines of ethical practice, which require all purchases and trades to increase the value of our own public collection. As you might suspect, to travel in that world requires one to be well informed about the market as a whole. I'm afraid my job description is a bit more pedestrian."

"It's all more complicated than I thought," he said. "To me, it's like a room full of doors, all opening into some other world."

"That describes it very well, Ethan, but be careful. You wouldn't be the first to get bitten by the rare book bug. It's quite fatal, you know. Our collection is astonishing, really, just extraordinary. There are rare and ancient books behind that door that have been personally signed by our earliest presidents and philosophers.

"We maintain an inventory of our titles in the office, if you'd care to see sometime. The collection has grown nicely under Dr. Morrigan's care, and donations have increased as a result. We've had notable collectors donate their entire personal libraries.

"Well, I must get back to work. Do you have any questions?"

He paused. "I have wondered what

happened to the person I'm replacing. If there was a problem, I'd as soon not repeat it."

"No problems at all, as far as anyone knows. He just up and left, not even a goodbye. You never can tell about people, I guess."

Chapter 10

Friday after lunch, Dr. Bates Morrigan tapped on his office door window and motioned for Anna to come in. A flush crept into her neck. Anytime she received personal attention from Dr. Morrigan, she wound up with more work to do.

Like any good archivist, Morrigan demanded perfection in all matters, which should have been a good thing, but it left him in a constant state of disappointment with the rest of humanity. Dr. Morrigan didn't abide error in others and was short on praise even in its absence. Anna had learned long ago that the best interaction with him was no interaction at all. Unfortunately, like today, that was not always possible.

"Close the door, Anna, and sit down," he said. "I've just come from a meeting with the library board, and it's their consensus that we presently don't have enough to do."

"Excuse me?" she said.

"The board feels that the library should organize and manage a public book club."

Anna looked up, knowing what was coming. "But there are already a number of book clubs in the community, Dr. Morrigan."

"But not a *public* book club, and not one sponsored by the library."

"There's a difference?" she asked.

"*Public,* like it says. Unlike private clubs, there are no rules about who can belong or how long they can stay. A *public* institution, supported by *public* funds, is obliged to have a *public* club. You do see the point? The city is concerned that our citizens cannot possibly survive without one."

Anna's breath shortened. There was no way out of it. "While that sounds interesting, I suppose, it would require a lot of time and effort, and as you know, we are short of help."

"This would require someone on staff to participate, Anna. You can imagine what an unsupervised club might look like. Our reputation is at stake here."

"People would love to hear from you personally, Dr. Morrigan. I mean, all the unique experiences you've had."

He rose and came around the table.

"You've heard the expression 'blowing smoke up someone's skirt,' I presume?"

"But Dr. Morrigan, perhaps someone in the community would be more qualified."

"No one in the community is the associate librarian. You are, Anna. This clearly falls under your job description. Now, you may use the Genealogy Room on the first floor for the meetings. We can arrange to have the floor open after hours, if needed."

"Dr. Morrigan—"

He held up his hand. "I want you to get it organized, post the meeting time on our bulletin board, and run it in the newspaper. Make sure there is a poster in the front window of the library as well. People in the community look up to you, Anna. All you have to do is get a few of them together and read a book. How hard can it be?"

"But, Dr. Morrigan . . . I mean, I'm not really prepared for something like this. I have a great deal of work lined up already for the library, and this would be after hours."

"You do know how to read and research, Anna, if I'm not mistaken. The rest is a simple matter of sharing a common experience, like reading the same damn book. I'm sure you can figure it out.

"Look, Anna, one does not join the library staff believing there will never be after-hour duties. The library will provide copies to anyone in the club who is not able to purchase a book. Let me know when you've made a decision about what titles you will be reading."

"But how do we select the title to read? No one wants to read the same book, not ever."

"There must be ample material out there on how to organize a book club. Find it. You are a librarian, I believe. Or just ask around. Private citizens do book clubs all the time."

Resigned, Anna dropped her arms to her sides. "So, when does this club have to start?"

"Soon. I don't want the board barking at me about this again, ever."

"What should I do first?"

Morrigan rolled his eyes and sat back down at his desk. "Select a name for the club."

"Yes, sir," she said, turning to leave.

"And tell that new janitor . . . what's his name?"

"Poser," she said. "Ethan Poser."

"Tell him that he's not to neglect the fiction aisles just because it's busy."

"I'll remind him," she said.

"And if you have any problems . . ."

"Like you said, Dr. Morrigan, I will figure it out."

***

That night, Anna checked out a stack of reference materials on how to organize a public book club. After reading for a couple of hours, she was convinced that organizing a political party might be easier. At least there, presumably, everyone would agree as to what party they belonged to. By definition, a public book club encompassed as many views as the public at large, which, in her experience, was too disparate to organize around anything, much less which books to read.

On top of that, she considered her own reading list as one of the few things in life that belonged to her alone and to no one else. Spending her evenings herding strangers through some dim book sounded perfectly dreadful.

She'd no sooner settled in with an iced tea when the phone rang. She'd forgotten to call her mother.

"Hello," she said.

"Anna, it's your mother."

"I just got home, Mother. I was going to call."

"It's all right, dear."

"It's just that I've been given another assignment at work, a book club to organize, and I had to do some reading on it."

"Read a book and talk about it, Anna. You've been doing that your whole life. What's to know, right?"

"Yes, I suppose."

"I was going through some old picture albums today. You remember the ones I've had on the top shelf in my closet."

"I remember."

"I came across some of Danny's pictures, you know the ones."

"Wearing the little hat."

"That one, and everything just came rushing back. You would think by now—"

"I really should get back to my work, Mother. Was there something in particular you needed?"

"No, no, I was just calling. It's all right for a mother to call her daughter, isn't it?"

"Of course it is. I didn't mean—"

"Well, I did stop by the cemetery on my way home."

"You saw the flowers?"

"The lilacs were beautiful. I'm so glad you took time out of your busy schedule."

"Thank you, Mother. If there's nothing else, I really need to get this finished before bedtime."

"Of course. So sorry to disturb you."

Anna spent the remainder of the evening reading the ins and outs of organizing book clubs and the myriad challenges for facilitators. Problems offered up concerned pushy personalities, not staying on topic, too much wine sipping, politics, religion, food competition, and not least was the endless dispute about which books a group would read.

Satisfied that she had been right in the first place, that this whole plan was going to be a giant fiasco, she went to bed. But sleep didn't come. She lay in the dark considering all the different interests people might have: romance, mystery, the classics, fantasy, sci-fi, westerns, mainstream, biography. There was no end, and then, which authors? How could she ask the entire group to read a single title and not expect anything less than war?

She turned onto her side and sighed. She should have been a tax accountant, or an attorney, like her father had wanted. Satisfying the public in a public institution was difficult at best. It came with a unique set of problems. There was an unspoken assumption of personal ownership among patrons, and rightly so, she supposed—though it often complicated matters for the staff. Situations arose that she could never have anticipated, disappointments that were antithetical to the rarefied atmosphere of a beautiful library.

    She got up and went to the window. The moon rose into the coal-black sky. She thought about Danny lying out there alone, about how he would have been a grown man by now. A call from her mother could bring with it unspoken and harsh messages. She knew in her heart that her mother had not forgiven her for Danny's death. How could she? She had not forgiven herself.

Chapter 11

On his way to work Monday morning, Ethan walked through the park and past the lake. It was a marginal park at best, old and well worn, with WPA-built restrooms and an old merry-go-round that leaned precariously to one side. Beer cans were scattered about, and a black plastic shopping bag hung from a tree limb like a sinister bat.

Few people were out and about that early in the morning—an old man with red whiskers walking his dog and a woman with her hat pulled low on her ears. He looked for the lady and little boy whom he'd seen earlier in the park, but they were nowhere to be found.

He was the first to arrive at the library and a little excited at having a key to the beautiful old building. He entered through the back door and shut off the security alarm, as Anna had shown him. By the time he'd located the lights and opened the front, both Dr. Morrigan and Anna had arrived. Anna waved with her fingertips on her way to the office.

He put his lunch in the desk in the basement shop and searched through the drawers: a half-melted chocolate bar, paper clips, an old *Playboy* magazine with the centerfold missing, a key ring with random keys attached. In the closet were a pair of work boots with the laces missing, and a fatigue jacket hung from a hook on the back of the door. It appeared that his predecessor had left in a hurry.

He started his first day on the first floor, as Anna had suggested. "Ground floor gets busy as the day goes on," she'd said. "The mezzanine is the least dirty and least busy. Our old custodian usually attended to it later in the day. I think he may have found a place for napping as well."

Ethan, determined to impress, worked steadily, pushing his giant dust mop through the aisles. Patrons moved aside, holding their books to their chests as he passed, but it was a mechanical response, like stepping back from a passing car, and not a greeting that acknowledged him in any personal way. He was part of the facility, faceless and silent, missed only if needed for something. He was going to have to adjust.

Throughout the day, he would see Anna busy with the patrons, leading them through the stacks, checking out their books at the desk. She moved from one person to the next, confident and knowledgeable. Many who came in sought her out, knowing from experience, or perhaps instinctively, that she was both competent and pleasant.

At times Ethan watched her covertly, catching glimpses of her now and again as she moved through the stacks, lifting onto her toes to reach for a book, her hair spilling down her back. He took in those moments, storing them away in his memory.

At noon he ate alone in the basement, the high window casting its dim light across the concrete floor. His lunch was cold and unappetizing, and he set aside the banana for a later time.

Kicking his feet up on the desk, he closed his eyes for a moment's rest, and that's when he heard something. It might have been the ancient plumbing clanking in the high reaches of the ceiling. Pipes threaded everywhere throughout the utility room like a giant metal octopus. He dropped his feet and listened. It came again, but from the furnace room. He opened the door to find a man sitting next to the furnace smoking a cigarette. He was big, with leather-colored skin and dark eyes, and the collar of his shirt was frayed with wear.

Ethan stepped back. "Hey, what are you doing? Who are you?"

The man stood and squashed his cigarette under his foot. "Who are *you*?"

"Ethan Poser, the new custodian. You didn't answer me."

The man looked over Ethan's shoulder to see if anyone else was around. "I am Diego."

"Diego who?"

"Diego Pinto."

"What are you doing in my shop?"

Diego pointed to the squashed butt on the floor. "Smoking."

"This area is for personnel only. You shouldn't be down here."

Diego looked at him, his eyes a liquid black. "There is no smoking in the library."

"This *is* the library."

"It is the old basement," he said.

"It is the library shop, and there's no smoking down here."

"There are no signs for smoking. I looked everywhere."

"I'm sorry, but it's against the rules."

Diego pointed his chin toward the stairs. "Dr. Morrigan does not complain when I smoke down here."

"Does he know?"

"Maybe."

"Look, Diego, I don't mean to be rude, but I could get into trouble letting you smoke in the library."

"Americans have many policemen," he said. "Diego, you must obey the rules even when there are no rules to see. Diego, no sleeping in the magazines. Diego, no sleeping on the library steps. Diego, you cannot look at women in the magazines. Diego, you cannot sleep in the books. Diego, do you steal maybe all the books?"

"I don't make the rules, Diego."

"The other custodian let me smoke, if I give him a cigarette. Do you want a cigarette, Ethan?"

"I don't smoke."

"I maybe bring a bottle of tequila for you. I can share with you."

"I cannot be bribed, Diego. It's against the rules."

"Do you have a sign, 'Ethan cannot be bribed'?"

"Look, it's just the way it is. I don't want to lose my job because you are addicted to tobacco."

"He did not hate immigrants."

"I don't hate immigrants. I just don't want you smoking down here."

"Maybe you break my civil rights, Ethan. It's against the law to hate immigrants who smoke. Everyone in America has the right to smoke. Maybe I'll report you to immigration authority and then you go to jail."

"I don't hate immigrants who smoke, or don't smoke, but I'm beginning to hate you."

"It's a rule not to hate," he said.

"This is personal, because you are going to cost me my job."

Diego followed Ethan out of the furnace room and paused at the desk. "You did not finish your lunch, Ethan."

"I did."

"You must not leave food to waste. It is a sin. Perhaps your hate has spoiled your appetite."

"I have finished my lunch."

"Not the banana. Bananas spoil very quickly, Ethan. If I had food wasting, I would give it to someone, even an immigrant."

"You want my banana. Is that what you're saying?"

"I am not hungry, but we must not let it waste."

"Fine, then. Eat the banana."

Diego sat down at the desk and peeled the banana. "You should buy them green. They last much longer that way."

"Why are you here in the library, Diego? Shouldn't you be at work or home or something?"

"Anna says the library is free for everyone. Anna does not hate immigrants like some people. She lets me read the newspaper in the big chair next to the magazines."

"You come to the library every day?"

"The library is closed on holy days."

"And you sit in the chair and read the newspaper?"

"Sometimes maybe I fall asleep, but only for a moment."

"It's against the rules to sleep in the library. You must know that."

"Sometimes the other custodian slept in history where no one goes."

"Where are you from, Diego?"

"I am a born-again United States citizen, but they have lost my records," he said, dropping the banana peel into the trash. "I see you soon, Ethan."

***

By the end of the day, Ethan's arms burned and feet ached. Custodial work had turned out to be more physical than he had anticipated. He washed in the downstairs restroom and checked his cleaning supplies. There was enough for a couple more days.

He closed up his shop and took the stairs to the mezzanine. It was his job to secure the library at night, and he was to make certain that everyone was gone before he locked the doors.

Special Collections was locked, and the stained glass windows in front lit with the lowering sun.

He worked his way back down to the first floor. Everyone had gone, or so he thought, until he spotted Anna emerging from the Genealogy Room.

"Hi," he said. "I thought everyone was gone."

She pushed her hair back with her fingers, her green eyes smiling. "I'm sorry I've kept you,

Ethan. I'm nearly finished. You see, I've been given the dubious honor of organizing a public book club for the library. Once organized, we will be conducting it after hours, I'm afraid."

"A what?"

"A *public* book club. I'm just learning about it, to tell the truth. It's like any book club, but free and open to the public at large. As a librarian, I'm fully aware of what free and open to the public entails."

"Fewer filters?" he said.

She smiled. "Well, when something is free . . . Have you ever belonged to a book club, being a teacher and all, I mean?"

"Too busy getting an education to read books," he said.

"Why don't you join us?"

"I'm the janitor, remember?"

"Think about it, Ethan. I'm looking for members. Dr. Morrigan wants this thing in operation yesterday."

"I'll keep it in mind," he said.

"Well, I'll get out of here so you can lock up. You're all settled in, I guess?"

He nodded. "Walking distance from home."

"Me as well. See you tomorrow, then."

He watched her descend the front steps

of the library, her copper hair sweeping about her face in the evening breeze. Her invitation to join the book club was at odds with his plans to find a better job, one that he could make into a lucrative career. If he were honest with himself, he was drawn to her. But he'd experienced firsthand how quickly things can turn. The pain of Olivia's deception was still raw in his memory, and he was not prepared to risk it, not with anyone, not ever again.

Chapter 12

Ethan quickly adjusted to the work and soon learned the faces of the regular patrons, some seeking refuge of one sort or another in the safety of the library. Others came in on a consistent schedule, including housewives, their arms overflowing with novels; college students, frantic over late homework; and the occasional senior citizen in search of some remote but celebrated ancestor.

    Despite Ethan's repeated warnings, Diego Pinto claimed the furnace room as his personal smoking zone, and soon Ethan was bringing an extra banana. Realizing the futility of trying to dissuade Diego of anything, he provided an ashtray and folding chair as well.

    Over the weeks, he'd discovered shortcuts to reduce the number of trips up and down the stairs, which in turn had lessened his leg cramps, which had resulted in a better night's rest. Even the camper, which bucked and pitched under the slightest breeze, felt more like home. There was a certain comfort and efficiency in its compactness. He seldom ate out because of the cost and so had improved his cooking skills as well. The greatest relief was the current but temporary absence of Dr. Morrigan, who had gone somewhere to appraise yet more rare books.

Overall, life was not so bad. Although Olivia's betrayal still haunted him, there were busy moments at work during which the ache faded. It would most often return in the hours he spent alone. In a way, he missed the whirl and drama of teaching, custodial work by definition being an isolating occupation. Even as he worked among the patrons, his obscurity was never in doubt.

Often he lingered at the locked door of the Special Collections room while cleaning the mezzanine. His lack of access to the collection had only heightened his curiosity about what lay inside. There were times his desire to enter rose inexplicably, an unreasonable craving, perhaps the same that drove so many collectors to irrational acts.

***

Friday came, and he was making his rounds to clear the library at closing time. As he passed the Genealogy Room, he heard voices inside. He could see Anna at the front of the room talking to two people.

"I don't mean to disturb," he said. "Will you be needing the front door kept unlocked this evening?"

Anna said, "Yes, please. We are having our first club meeting. I'll make certain to secure everything before I leave. Dr. Morrigan gave permission to keep it open for the meetings."

"Right," he said. "Good night, then."

"Oh, before you go, let me introduce you to some of the founding members of our new book club. This lady here is Doris Gill. Doris, this is Ethan Poser."

Ethan nodded. Doris was a heavyset, older woman, in her seventies probably. She wore a sweater, a bit too large, and her glasses hung on the end of her nose. She studied him over their tops with slate-gray eyes.

"Nice to meet you," Ethan said.

Doris nodded and pushed her glasses up. "Just think what you might learn in the club, Ethan."

"I could use some *learnin'*," he said, smiling.

"And this is Mia Layla," Anna said. "She tells me she is an avid reader and so wants to join the group."

"Hello," Ethan said.

Mia was young, way young for such a book club, he thought, maybe in her early twenties, even younger. She tipped her head, like a kitten might, and reached out for his hand.

"Hi," she said. "Please do consider joining us."

"I'm sure it would be interesting. I will give it some thought. Well, nice meeting everyone."

"Good night," Anna said. "If you change your mind, do let me know, Ethan. We'd love to have you in the group."

***

The sun was an orange flare churning below the horizon as he made his way home. Shadows stretched out from the trees and moved in the evening breeze. The park was deserted of people that time of day. A flock of crows, like nuns in habits, gathered on the merry-go-round. The sunset reflected in the water of the small lake, and waves rippled onto the shore.

Reluctant to go back to his camper just

yet, Ethan walked out onto the rickety pier and sat down to enjoy the last of the day. The waves sloshed gently against the pillars, and the faint smell of moss scented the air.

He thought about Anna, the way she took on her work with such determination. The book club would be a lot for her, and with little compensation. But he figured she would give it all she had anyway. He was certain that it was character, not money, that drove Anna in her dedication to the library.

He stood to leave but froze when he spotted something moving in the water. At first he thought it a fish, dead and belly-up. It was not a fish, but an arm, bloated with water. The hand, gray and strutted, undulated in the waves, a macabre greeting as the body floated toward him. With each incoming swell, it rolled and tugged against the rope that entangled it. The hand waved silently up at him as the body drifted beneath the pier.

Ethan's throat tightened, and his breath grew shallow. He gathered himself up against the anxiety that had swept through him. Dropping down onto his stomach, he peered between the boards for a closer look, but by then the sun had sunk below the horizon, and only shadows and blackness were below. But as his eyes slowly adjusted, he could make out the rope that was entangled on a pillar and held the body in place.

He sat back on his heels, his heart pounding. Maybe it was a bum, or a drug deal gone bad. This was a small park, and security was scant at best. Maybe it was a heart attack, a fisherman, a boating accident. Things happened. People died for all kinds of reasons every day, and often alone. But then, who knew what deeds might go on in that park at night? Who really knew the bodies that might lie beneath the waters?

His first inclination was to leave. No one would ever know that he'd been there. The park was vacant. But what if the person beneath the pier was still alive, unconscious, stilled by the cold water and in need of assistance? What if he wasn't dead but struggling to hang on, desperate for someone to save him? But then, anyone could see that he was dead, bloated, silent, and pale. But what if? How could he leave someone to drown?

He eased himself over the side of the pier and into the chilly water. His legs cramped, and he gasped for breath. Holding on to the edge of the pier, he reached under and grabbed the arm, stiff with rigor mortis. He knew his first impression had been right. This guy was dead, had been for some time.

The body lifted with an incoming wave. There was a sound. Chills raced down Ethan's back, and his stomach knotted. He should call someone, report it. But if he did, then what? He'd be implicated in a situation he really had nothing to do with. He'd walked out on a pier, that's all, and suddenly he was involved in an unexplained death. Innocent people were dragged into these kinds of situations all the time. One second, all is well with the world, a beautiful sunset on a beautiful evening. The next second, his reputation is ruined, his job gone, even worse, all because he had been in the wrong place at the wrong time. No one would believe him. No one would care that he was just trying to do the right thing here. They'd be looking for someone to blame.

He worked his way back onto shore, pausing to see if he was still alone. The crows had flown off into a nearby tree for the night and watched him in silence. It was too late to help this guy now. He was someone else's problem. There was no one to know what he'd discovered under that pier, no one to know he'd been there and had left without explanation. Turning up his collar, he moved off into the darkness toward home.

Chapter 13

The camper was a coffin, crowded and airless. He lay in the darkness, reliving what he'd seen under that pier. He'd known death before, but at a safe distance. This had been up close and personal. Like it or not, he was involved, maybe even implicated—maybe, God forbid, would be held responsible.

He struggled to shake those thoughts from his mind. Why hadn't he contacted the authorities? It was the right thing to do. Now there were lies and deceit. He and the dead man were forever linked. One minute, he's walking home from a hard day's work. The next minute, he's connected to a suspicious death, perhaps even a murder, the cruelest of human endeavors.

Some time in the night, he sat up on the side of his bed. He could see the moon through the kitchen window, a blood-red orb suspended in the blackness, and beyond, the shadow of the vacant house on the street. Someone could have been in there, watching him as he made his way from the park to the camper. In his heart, he knew that what he'd done could no longer be denied. Sooner or later, he was going to have to own it.

He dressed in the darkness and slipped on a jacket before striking out for the park. It was empty and silent, as he knew it would be. The red moon had faded into ginger against the stars. He paused at the pier and looked about. Slipping off his shoes, he stepped into the coldness of the lake. A car honked somewhere off in the distance, followed by an angry squeal of tires as it sped away. Chills raced up his back and settled into his shoulders as he moved beneath the pier.

The body was still there, as he knew it would be, anchored in its watery grave. He opened his pocketknife and sawed at the water-soaked rope. The body moved against his leg, and he shivered at its touch. Steeling himself, he took its arm, stiff and cold, and worked his way toward shore, pulling the corpse behind. He could feel its resistance, its reluctance to be dragged ashore for all to see.

Suddenly, from out of nowhere, pulsing red-and-blue lights lit up the night. A man stepped forward, his sidearm leveled at Ethan. "Climb on out of there," he said. "You're under arrest."

***

Hours later, Captain Kane Armen sat across from Ethan. He leaned back in his office chair and pulled at his bottom lip. He was dressed in uniform, his hair graying at the temples, and a dab of shaving cream hung under his ear. Rolling his chair forward, he hooked his elbows on the desk.

He looked to Ethan like someone out of a World War II movie. Ethan twisted sideways in his chair. His wrists ached from the handcuffs, and he struggled to relax under their claustrophobic grip. He lowered his head against the stress and the stiffness that had wormed into his shoulders and neck. He'd never been detained before, not ever, and to be in someone's total control was frightening. His inability to resist, even to stand without permission, caused him to burn inside with weakness and rage.

Captain Armen studied him, his eyes like glass. "What's your name?" he asked.

"Ethan Poser."

Captain Armen turned his chair to the side and wove his fingers together. "Well, Ethan Poser, you've had yourself quite a night. Where are you from?"

Where *was* he from? Ethan couldn't remember. "Here," he said. "I'm from here."

"Funny thing that, Ethan Poser. I don't believe I've ever seen you before. What you doing here?"

"I was a teacher."

"Was?"

"A temporary teacher at the high school."

"You ever been in trouble before, Ethan?"

"No, sir."

"Never been arrested?"

"Never."

"We can check that easy enough. Know the first thing a troublemaker does, don't you?" Ethan shook his head. "He lies. The thing is, after all the years doing this job, I can spot a liar a mile off, and ain't nothing pisses me off more."

"I'm not lying, sir."

"You *was* a teacher, but now you ain't?"

"That's right."

The captain stood, leaning in on the desk with his hands. "So, with no job and no money coming in, you decided to mug someone in the park. Ain't that right? It got out of hand, and you wound up killing him, accidently, of course?"

"No, sir, it didn't happen that way. I have a new job. I have money, and I would never kill anyone."

"What kind of new job do you have?"

"I work at the library."

He stood and folded his arms. "You're a librarian?"

"I'm the custodian."

He rolled up his chair, sat back down, and studied Ethan. "Bit of a demotion, isn't it?"

"It's honest work."

"How did you come to know about this custodian job? How did you know that the previous custodian was no longer working there?"

"I just happened to see the help wanted sign in the library office window."

"So, you went to the library and just happened upon this job, accidently like? Do I have that right?"

Ethan nodded. "I needed the work. I saw the sign. I asked about the job and got it."

"You didn't know before that the other custodian had just walked away, had suddenly disappeared?"

"Someone may have mentioned it later."

"It was just a coincidence that you showed up for his job shortly after his disappearance?"

"I happened to see the sign. I figured it to be better than no job at all. Look, I've nothing to do with any of this. I just stumbled onto that body on my way home."

"About what time did you just stumble upon this body?"

"Probably six or so. I was on my way back and decided to go out on the pier."

Captain Armen looked at the piece of paper in front of him. "It says here that the police arrested you at three a.m. while you were engaged in pulling a corpse out of the lake. How do you explain that, Mr. Poser?"

"I came back to the pier later on," he said.

"But why?"

"I couldn't sleep."

"And what were you going to do when you got back to the pier?"

"I don't know exactly."

"But when you got there, you decided to go into the water and pull out the body? Would that be correct?"

Sweat ran into Ethan's eyes. "To tell the truth, when I first found the body, I just didn't want to get involved."

"Involved?"

"Like now, like being asked these questions and being accused of something I didn't do."

"But then, in the middle of the night, you decided to get involved anyway, is that right?"

"Yes."

"You own a gun, Mr. Poser?"

"No, I don't."

"A .38 caliber perhaps?"

"No."

"We've found a .38 slug in the guy you pulled out of the lake in the middle of the night. Now, suppose you tell me where that gun is."

"I don't own a gun."

"Where exactly do you live, Mr. Poser?"

"In a camper on Fifth, in an RV park."

"Close to the lake?"

"Close to the library."

"Are you married?"

"No."

"Ever been?"

"No. Look, what does this have to do with anything? I was on my way home after work and stopped at the lake pier to sit a bit. That's when I saw the body."

"And then you went on home like nothing had happened?"

"Yes, but—"

"And your conscience was hurting, so you got up at three in the morning and went back to do something, but we don't know exactly what?"

"I know it sounds crazy," Ethan said.

"You don't know a Clarence Belowe, Mr. Poser?"

"No," he said. "Who's that?"

"Clarence Belowe is the name on the driver's license that we found in the dead man's wallet, the man you were dragging to shore at three a.m. We made calls."

"I've never heard of Clarence Belowe. What are you trying to say?"

"Clarence Belowe was the custodian at the library, the man whose job you took."

"I just took a job that was open. I don't understand."

"Nor I, Mr. Poser, but I'm not a big believer in coincidence, you see. I've been a policeman far too long for that."

Captain Armen tapped his index finger on the paper in front of him. "Clarence Belowe suddenly disappears from his job and for no apparent reason. You, coincidentally, show up a week later and apply for said job. Then, the biggest coincidence of all, we find you dragging his body out of the lake at three in the morning. You do see the problem?"

"You think I'd shoot a man in the back just so that I could take his job—a custodian's job at that?"

"Did I say *back*? I don't believe I did, but you are correct. That's exactly where we found the slug—yet another coincidence."

"I just thought that . . ."

Captain Armen got up and walked to the window. He was a large man, older than Ethan had first thought. His hair was thinning in the back. "I'm going to release you for now, Mr. Poser, but you are not to leave town. This investigation is not over. Do you understand?"

"Yes, sir."

"You see, murder cannot be covered up for long. There will be evidence to come. There always is, so if you have something to say, now is the time to say it."

"I'm innocent," Ethan said.

"My advice is to get yourself a good lawyer. You are going to need one; meanwhile, do not leave the city."

"I'm free to go?"

"*Free* is not exactly the word I'd choose, Mr. Poser."

Chapter 14

Arriving hours late for work, Ethan noted the light shining from Dr. Morrigan's office. He must have returned from his collections trip. Before he could sneak past to the basement shop, Dr. Morrigan emerged and, spotting Ethan, motioned for him to come into his office.

"Close the door," Morrigan said. "This library has been neglected. Do you have an explanation?"

"Yes, sir, I do."

Dr. Morrigan's eyes narrowed. "Well?"

"I was walking home after work and stopped at the pier, the one at the park lake. I saw . . . I discovered a body under the pier."

Morrigan stood. "Did you say *body*?"

"A man. He was caught up in the water with a rope. I was shocked, you see, afraid I'd become involved in something. So, I left, but later that night I went back. I decided to retrieve the body, and I was going to contact the police."

"And?"

"I didn't have a chance. I was arrested there. I've been trying to make someone understand ever since." Ethan rubbed his damp hands on his pants. "The thing is . . . the thing is, the body was one Clarence Belowe, apparently the custodian who used to work here."

Morrigan looked up through his brows. "Good God, you found Clarence Belowe's body in the park lake?"

Ethan nodded. "Someone killed him, shot him in the back, and no one knows who or why. No money was taken from his wallet. No motive. No witnesses have come forward."

"And you are now implicated in this? This reflects on all of us, you know. Library patrons have a right to feel safe, Mr. Poser, to be safe."

"All I did was spot the body under the pier. I was uncertain, spooked, really, and I left. And then when I tried to make it right, the whole thing blew up. Now I'm in over my head. I'm really sorry, Dr. Morrigan."

"Have you been charged with anything?"

"No. Not yet, but they might. It was a stupid thing I did, a mistake."

"How do they know it was Clarence Belowe?"

"They recovered his driver's license."

"We hardly knew him here at the library," he said. "He'd worked only a short while when he just disappeared. The scandal . . . the police . . . they will be coming here, I suppose?"

"Captain Armen said the investigation is ongoing."

"I don't want this spread around unnecessarily. This sort of thing could be ruinous to Special Collections. We depend heavily on contributions, you know. Collectors are quite protective of their books, even as they surrender them to the library. They won't abide something like this, not for a minute."

"I'll do what I can, Dr. Morrigan, but this really has nothing to do with me. All I did was discover the body. I'm afraid this is bound to come out at some point."

Morrigan turned. "All right, Poser. That will be all, for now."

"Dr. Morrigan, about my job?"

"We'll see, I suppose. In the meantime, get this place cleaned up."

***

Avoiding Anna, Ethan started on the first floor like always, but it was getting toward midafternoon, and his work was slow, compounded by his own emotional state. He had managed to get on the wrong side of Morrigan within a few short days of being employed, and Morrigan was not one to tolerate mistakes. But it was all out of his control now.

Not only was he personally stressed by what had happened but the facility's condition had deteriorated in his brief absence. He was only the custodian, to be sure, but he'd taken a lot of pride in keeping everything tip-top. The waste baskets were running over, and someone had eaten a pizza in Periodicals.

By the time he'd made it up to the mezzanine, it was getting late. He'd struggled to concentrate on his work, but the image of Belowe's waterlogged corpse kept rushing back.

He finished cleaning upstairs and was gathering up supplies when he noticed a light coming from under the Special Collections door. It was unusual for anyone to be in Special Collections that late in the day, even Morrigan, who on occasion stayed over to finish up work or meet with the collections board. Ethan tried the doorknob. It was locked, so he continued on to the basement to put away his supplies.

It was on his way out that he noticed the

Genealogy Room door ajar. He could see Anna deeply involved in a book. He'd managed to avoid her most of the day. She was surely aware of his absence, and what was he to tell her?

She looked up, her ginger hair falling across an eye. "Oh, Ethan," she said, "I'm running late. What time is it?"

"Late," he said. "I'm closing up now."

She shut her book and retrieved her jacket from behind the door. "I'm sorry. I became involved with this book we've selected for the club. Time got away."

She waited in the hall for him to turn off the main lights and lock up. As they made their way to the back, Ethan could smell her vanilla perfume and see the curve of her hips against the hallway exit light. He waited for her to step out before setting the alarm. He double-checked the lock behind him.

"Ethan," she said, "I don't mean to interfere, but I couldn't help noticing that you have been avoiding me. Is everything OK?"

"Are you walking or driving?" he asked.

"Walking. I usually cut through the park. It's shorter that way."

"May I walk with you?"

She paused and looked at him with those jade-green eyes, and for the briefest moment he forgot what he'd just asked her.

She took his arm. "I'd like that," she said. "I find walking easier than trying to find a parking space, don't you?"

"You should be careful walking in the park after dark, Anna."

"I usually don't this late, but the book club meeting was coming up. I needed to make some notes. The time just got away from me."

"Ah, the book club," he said. "How is that coming?"

"Slow, but we are gaining. We're up to three members now. Imani Bell, a woman from across town, has joined. She's retired from the phone company, nice but reticent. I'm hoping she'll warm up and participate."

They walked on into the park itself. He could feel her at his side, her silence and warmth. As they approached the pier, Anna stopped and looked over at him. "Ethan, what's going on? You can tell me."

He could see the lake behind her and hear the gentle slosh of the waves beneath the pier.

"I promised Dr. Morrigan I wouldn't talk about it, Anna."

"Are you in some kind of trouble?"

"Maybe."

"Ethan, what's this about? You have my promise. I won't say a word to anyone."

"It's ridiculous, really. Walking home after work, I went out on the pier, that pier, to enjoy the moment, you know. I spotted something."

"You spotted something?"

"A body. It had washed up under the pier."

Anna covered her mouth and turned to look. "There was a body under the pier?"

"They say it was Clarence Belowe."

"Oh my goodness, *our* Clarence, from the library?"

He nodded. "I panicked and left without reporting it. I didn't want to get involved. But later that night I decided I had no choice but to go back. The police showed up." He took a deep breath. "They arrested me and took me in for interrogation. It was all just so crazy."

"How awful. Poor Clarence. I barely knew him, but he used to come into the library on occasion before he was hired. He liked to browse, you know, and he was always friendly."

"I had nothing to do with any of this, Anna. Like a fool, I left without reporting it. I was afraid of becoming entangled in something. But my conscience was hurting me, so I came back. I thought I had to do the right thing. I don't think they believed me."

They walked on toward the swings. Anna pulled up. "That's extraordinary, Ethan. You have no idea. For that to happen here in this very park." She shuddered. "I wonder how many times I walked by it?"

He described to her then what he'd seen, how he'd pulled the corpse onto shore and how the police had arrived out of the night.

"The body was bloated with water," he said, shivering. "The police said he'd been shot in the back."

"Poor Clarence," she said. "He was such a solitary soul. It doesn't make sense, Ethan. Why would someone kill him? He couldn't have had money."

"I don't know," he said.

"It's such a sad and lonely place to die."

They walked on, and when they'd reached the RV park, Ethan stopped. "This is where I live, in there. It's home—in a fashion, I mean."

"I can walk by myself from here, Ethan. It's not far."

"I'd better go with you. I mean, with all this going on, I would feel better."

She took his hand. "OK. It *is* a little scary, I admit."

A few blocks on, Anna pointed out a small frame house tucked back in the trees. It was older but had been carefully maintained. The yard was manicured, and flowers were planted in every available space. "There," she said, "that's my place."

"You're right, we *are* neighbors."

She looked back at the way they'd come. "Would you like to come in for a drink? We can have it outside. I have a grand screened-in porch, and it's really pleasant this time of evening."

"Are you sure? It's been a long day."

She nodded. "A glass of wine?"

"Well, yes," he said. "I'd like that, and the company as well. I admit to feeling a little bruised up from Captain Armen's interrogation."

She held the screen door open and waited for him to go in. "Find a place to sit, and I'll get our wine. It's private and cool out here, and we can relax. I'll be right back."

As he waited for Anna's return, he could hear the crickets from the depths of the hedgerow that ran the length of the southern exposure, a cacophony of sounds casting into the night. The stars spilled across the universe, and the evening smelled of earth and dampness. He was glad that she'd invited him in, but uneasy at the same time. He could feel himself relaxing with her, preferring her company. He'd been there before in his life, and he must be cautious.

When Anna returned with their wine, she took up the wicker chair across from him. Pulling her legs under her, she tucked them modestly to the side. She sipped at the rim of her glass and ran the tip of her tongue over her lips to savor the rich Chianti. Her profile, all shadows and light, was like a flawless pencil sketch.

"Ethan," she said, setting down her glass, "I know so little about you."

"Well, what would you like to know?"

"Just stuff, I suppose. Were you always a perfect child?"

"Yes, of course, except for an occasional relapse."

"And brilliant as well, I'm assuming."

He took a drink of wine and shrugged. "Yes, I think brilliant sums it up. But I was a doubtful teacher, at least that's what my students led me to believe. Oh, I had moments of inspiration, but they were rarely appreciated."

She smiled. "And were you a popular boy as well, the kind the girls giggled over?"

He hooked his chin over his thumbs. "Frankly, I was probably everything your parents ever warned you about."

"Hmm," she said, smiling, "I suspected as much."

"And what about you, Anna?"

"Me? Well, let me see. I've been described as an ardent dreamer and romantic, someone who prefers living in her head rather than in the real world."

"I can see that," he said.

"I've been referred to as aloof on occasion, which couldn't be further from the truth. I see myself as having all the earmarks of a trendsetter. Of course, Mother says I have all the characteristics of a spinster."

"I think I might disagree with your mother."

"I wouldn't recommend disagreeing with my mother about anything," she said.

They talked into the evening as the moon sank behind the drifting clouds. From the hedgerow, the crickets' intense song mellowed, the tempo slowing for the night ahead.

Anna refilled their glasses, again and yet again, and they were soon settled into the comfort of the evening. She told him then of her brother's death, of his own drowning in that very same park lake, and how she had been haunted by it all these many years.

"And then for this to happen to Clarence Belowe, and in the same place," she said. "I feel like it's all my fault again somehow."

"How awful, Anna. I'm so sorry. I shouldn't have brought it up. I had no idea this happened to you. I was thinking of myself. I just needed to talk to someone. I didn't think it through. I didn't have the right to lay it at your feet like that."

"No, it's OK, Ethan. We all need to talk sometimes. Anyway, how were you to know?"

"I just didn't realize how personal this might be for you."

"It's the world's way of keeping us humble, I guess," she said.

For a while afterward, they sat in silence, contemplating the secrets they had just shared. What he hadn't said to her was how he wished he could take her into his arms, feel her warmth and the beat of her heart against him. He hadn't told her how empty and broken he was, nor how fearful of repeating the mistakes in his life. Instead, he listened, because it was what she needed most, and what he could most safely give.

Chapter 15

When Ethan arrived at work the next morning, he scoured the papers in the hope of finding more information about the discovery of Clarence Belowe's corpse. He found only a short entry on the second page. It stated that the police had recovered the body of an elderly man in the city park lake who had been shot in the back. Though foul play was clearly indicated, no arrests had yet been made. Anyone having information concerning the incident should contact Captain Kane Armen at the Sheriff's Department.

    Ethan reread the article, which he thought lacked a certain enthusiasm. Belowe was, after all, just a janitor, Ethan thought, probably what some considered a man of limited importance in the scheme of things. Even as a suspect himself, Ethan had been released rather quickly. Could they have had someone else in mind, or were they tailing him without his knowledge? They could have someone else in custody by now, for all he knew.

He'd no sooner finished cleaning the ground floor and sat down for his lunch when Diego Pinto came in. For someone living on the street, Diego was always shaved and perfectly clean. His routine at the library was consistent and quiet. He never interrupted or caused any kind of disturbance, save for his frequent trips to his favorite smoking area. Though he picked daily the material to read and went through it systematically, it wasn't always clear that he was reading at all. Sometimes he would mark his page before going to the restroom, or put his hat atop a book that he was reading, all to make sure that everyone knew that it was *his* material and that he would soon be back for it. Once, when Ethan was cleaning the area, he noticed that Diego's book was upside down.

"Hey, *amigo*," Diego said. "Are you still hiding from the police? This will be the first place they will look."

Ethan leaned back in his chair and shook his head. Diego had a pack of cigarettes turned into the sleeve of his shirt.

"What does that mean, Diego? I'm not hiding from anyone."

"I heard they found the body of Clarence Belowe floating in the park lake."

"I don't know what you're talking about."

"That's a good answer, Ethan. Never give too much, especially if your skin is brown."

Ethan rolled his eyes. "Who is this Clarence Belowe?"

"The old custodian who worked here, the nice one who let me smoke in the basement."

"I know nothing of Clarence Belowe. The job was open. I took it."

"The street says many things, Ethan."

"The street?"

"The street is more right than all policemen. If you want to know, ask the street. They know even when you cheat on your wife."

"I don't have a wife."

"So, there is one less sad woman in America."

Ethan glanced up through his brows. He couldn't always tell if Diego was serious or joking.

"And now you're going to give me advice about my love life, I suppose?"

"Latinos have great skill in such things, Ethan, but we would both be old before I could teach it to you."

Ethan said, "Your life is in more jeopardy than you might know, Diego. OK, so what does the street have to say about me?"

"That it was the new custodian who found Clarence Belowe's body and that he was arrested and taken in for questioning."

"It's only a rumor, and telling rumors is not good for the library or my job. If I lose my job, you will have no place to smoke, and what would you do?"

Diego looked around. "Maybe if I was not so hungry, I could forget these things. Have you forgotten your banana, Ethan?"

"I thought I might eat it myself for once."

"Sure, sure. It's OK to be greedy. I wouldn't tell the police you are hiding here, even though I'm hungry. You are my friend, and I would never tell because they might beat you."

"I'm not hiding, Diego. I am working, or I was. If I were hiding, you would not be able to find me, I assure you."

"This is the first place the police will look for you, for sure. Where can we find Ethan? I wonder if he would be in the library where he works. You see, maybe?"

"But I have no reason to hide."

"This is a good thing to always say. But when you do hide, there is an old shed down on the creek. The police never go there. It is too far to walk."

"I just happened to find a body under the pier, Diego. That's all. I'm not hiding from anyone."

Diego fished out a cigarette and lit up. Smoke curled upward into the shaft of light that came from the window.

Ethan waved the smoke from his face. "If Anna catches you smoking, you will have no place to lay up all day. What then?"

Diego tipped his chin. "It's only a little smoke. I have not killed anyone, Ethan. You should not call the pot and kettle black."

"This isn't about me. It's about you breaking the rules."

"I think Anna will let me smoke here because there are no signs to say stop smoking here, and because she has great interest for me."

"I didn't know."

"I have seen how she watches me from behind her desk."

"Really?"

"You should not be jealous of Latino love skills, Ethan. We have practiced them for many generations. Women know this, but I will not steal her from you, even if you do not bring bananas."

"Have you thought to buy your own bananas, Diego? It is the custom in America."

"But you are my friend, and I think you would not let me go hungry. But don't worry, I would never steal Anna away or tell the policeman where you are hiding."

"Well, if you're absolutely starving, there is a banana in my desk drawer. I hope you enjoy it."

Diego found the banana and took up the chair in front of the desk. "You know," he said, his mouth full, "I have been thinking."

"About what?"

"That I should join Anna's book club."

Ethan looked up. "What?"

Diego took another bite of banana. "There is a girl who has joined this club. Her name is Mia. Sometimes she smiles at me."

"A book club is for reading books, Diego. You do not join one because there is a pretty girl in it."

"Oh, I read many books, very big books. I was known in Mexico for such things. Sometimes there was no place for sitting in my house because of so many big books."

"Really, I had no idea. Look, you can't be bothering the patrons just because you want to be around a pretty girl. The book club members are there to read and to have intellectual discussions."

Diego reached for another cigarette and hooked it in the corner of his mouth. "Is this club only for those who can pay? I know that money is most important in America."

"It's a *public* club."

"Then anyone who is public can join without paying?"

"Yes."

"Even immigrants?"

"Even immigrants, but it matters to join because you really want to read books, not just annoy the pretty girls."

"That is me, for sure. I want to so much I can't sleep for wanting to. That is why I fall asleep sometimes in the magazines."

"Look, Diego, I'm not doubting your motivation, but these people are interested in literature."

"I love literature almost as much as bananas, and I promise to not steal away Anna or the girl, Mia."

"What's the last book you read?"

Diego pulled at his chin. "The name does not come to me. It was a very big name."

"OK, Diego, put out the cigarette. You need to go now. I've work to do."

Diego stubbed his cigarette and followed Ethan up the stairway. At the top, he paused and said, "Don't worry, Ethan, I have too many women to choose from."

***

That afternoon, Ethan was making a final pass of the mezzanine with his dust mop when he saw Dr. Morrigan coming out of Special Collections. Instinctively, he stepped back from sight and waited until Morrigan had disappeared down the stairs. He'd learned over the short time he'd worked at the library that it was better not to encounter Morrigan unless absolutely necessary. The fact that Morrigan was unhappy about the bad publicity had made that doubly important.

He was headed for the basement when Anna signaled him over to the checkout desk.

"There's someone waiting for you in your shop, Ethan," she said.

"Someone for me? Who?"

"A Captain Armen from the Sheriff's Department." She closed her book and stood. "Ethan . . ."

"It's all right, Anna. He's probably just wanting to clear up some things."

***

Captain Armen was sitting at Ethan's desk, his legs crossed and his hat hanging off the toe of his shoe.

"Mr. Poser," he said, removing his hat and dropping his leg. "Suppose I could talk to you for a moment?"

Ethan sat down. "You're giving me an option?"

Armen ran his fingers through his hair and smiled. "It won't take long, Poser. You see, we've had some new information come to light about your predecessor, the late Clarence Belowe, and we thought perhaps you might be able to help us out."

"Look, Captain, I don't really know anything about all this. I just happened to discover the body, unfortunately."

"It won't take long," he said. "You might recall that a .38-caliber bullet was recovered from Clarence Belowe's corpse by our forensics team?"

"Yes, someone mentioned that."

"What you probably didn't know was that Clarence Belowe's phone was recovered from the lake that same day by one of our divers."

"No, I wasn't aware of that."

"The phone was water damaged, as you might guess, but our forensic people are quite remarkable. They were able to glean some useful information."

"What kind of data are we talking about, Captain?"

"Primarily the date and time that the phone ceased to operate, which would have been most likely the time of his death, wouldn't it? Quite extraordinary how they do all that nowadays."

"But what does all this have to do with me?"

"Simply put, we need to know where you were at that time and on that date. If you can successfully establish that, we will reconsider charging you with the murder of Clarence Belowe."

Ethan sat back in his chair, heat rushing into his face. "How can you expect me to do that?"

"That's not my problem, is it?"

"What date, what time are we talking about here?"

"May sixth, five thirty p.m."

"I can't know something like that. Even if I did, how would I prove it? Do you know where you were?"

"*I* don't need to know."

Ethan dabbed the moisture from his upper lip with his sleeve. "Wait a minute. That was the last day of school and the last day of my job. I signed my classroom key in with the school secretary that day. She should be able to verify it."

"We will check it out."

"And then I'm cleared?"

"Let's say that you'll be better off, but there's still reason to believe that you could be withholding information from the police about Belowe, which is not a good thing, not good at all. I'll be in touch."

***

Ethan was on his way out when Anna motioned him over. "Is everything OK, Ethan?"

"Yes, I think so. He wanted some clarification was all."

"Ethan, I've noticed Diego Pinto going to your shop on several occasions. You might want to keep an eye on things. He seems like a nice man, but you never know."

"He thinks my shop is his private smoking lounge."

"We are having our club meeting tonight, and he's asked to join. I don't mind but, the thing is, I've never seen him actually read a book. I'm a little surprised that he's interested in the club."

"Maybe he's lonesome or something. You can never know what motivates people."

"No, I suppose not."

"Would you like for me to wait for you tonight?"

"You don't mind?"

"I'll be on the mezzanine."

Chapter 16

The mezzanine was a beautiful area with five surrounding chambers and a spectacular stained glass dome. At the east end was an enormous fireplace that had never been in use. The clatter of the world was silenced on the mezzanine, save for the beat of one's heart.

The Special Collections room occupied the entire north exposure of the floor, with its priceless volumes locked and secured at all times. Ethan had wondered how it must feel to explore those sacred stacks, to read and know those thoughts written so long ago. He imagined how it must be to converse with the spirits of the past and discover their long-held secrets.

It was eight o'clock by the time he heard Anna's footsteps as she climbed the stairs to meet him. She carried her notebook in her arms and her purse over her shoulder. Sitting down next to him, she sighed. Her scent that day was citrus, a happy and airy fragrance that suited her way with the world. The mellow lights from the dome scattered over her hair and in her eyes. Being alone with Anna lifted him up and made him feel braver than he was.

"Whew," she said. "Finally a little progress. We now have six members, counting me, and guess who?"

"Diego Pinto," he said.

She smiled. "He's actually quite charming, you know, if not a bit mischievous."

"Diego inhabits his own private space in the universe, that's certain."

"He does seem to be quite taken with Mia."

"And so things are coming together for the club, you think?"

"We've been getting organized, such a diverse group of people. I hope I can keep them gathered up. Folks can be quite emotional about their books."

"There is one advantage to being a simple custodian," he said. "I clean. That's my day."

"Right now, that sounds comforting, Ethan. It wasn't easy, but we did agree on how to select what books to read. That's a milestone, I'd say."

"Right up there with world diplomacy. So how does this work?"

"Each member of the club chooses a book they have enjoyed. At some point we will all read that book and then discuss it at the meeting. The person whose book is scheduled will be the leader of the discussion for that particular session."

"And?"

"And so we drew names to determine the order of the presentations. Guess who goes first?"

"Who?"

"Diego Pinto."

"You know, Anna, as the group leader, perhaps it would be better for you to choose the books and conduct the sessions yourself."

"Why would I do that? I want them to participate. It's important, Ethan."

"It's just that . . . I mean, *you* are the expert. Turning control over to the group is risky, isn't it?"

"It's what we agreed to do, Ethan. I'm sure Diego will do just fine."

"Yes, I'm sure. Well, perhaps we should be on our way home."

***

As they walked into the evening, Anna took his arm. The park, dimly lit under the antiquated lighting, stretched out ahead of them. Anna was silent, but content in her silence, as she could be.

The merry-go-round lay ahead, hunkered in the moonlight like an old dinosaur. Bent and worn from a thousand frantic rides, it leaned into the darkness. And the pier, with its soft lapping of waves and its faint smell of fish, stretched off into the water. A gull perched on the distant edge, a sentinel against the evil that had transpired there.

Anna's hand tightened on his arm. "So much loss here," she said, more to herself than to him. She looked up, her eyes dewy in the moonlight. "You've not really said what the captain wanted with you. Is there something you should share with me?"

"They were able to determine the day and time of Clarence Belowe's death by his phone, which was water damaged during the incident. Fortunately, I'm sure my whereabouts are established during that time. In short, I have a workable alibi."

"That's wonderful, Ethan! Then you are no longer under suspicion of anything?"

"I'm not entirely sure. You see, Captain Armen does *not* convince easily. So much of this is due to my poor judgment, I know. I knew better than to leave that night. I knew it wasn't the right thing to do, but I did it anyway. They have a right to be suspicious, I suppose."

They walked on to the merry-go-round and paused there. A threadbare path encircled it, worn from generations of feet. Anna sat down, and he joined her. In the distance was the faint glimmer of the city lights.

"Forgiving oneself is the hardest of all, I think," she said.

"Yes," he said. "We can be the hardest on ourselves sometimes. There's no hiding from the truth, I guess."

"I was just a young girl when Danny drowned," she said.

He took her hand. "I'm sorry that happened to you, Anna."

"I was left to watch him, you see, such a simple thing, really. But I failed, and the price of failure turned out be high. After all these years, and still . . ."

"You were just a kid yourself, Anna. You should never have been given that kind of responsibility. It wasn't your fault."

"I just forgot, you know, having fun I suppose, and when I looked up, he was gone. I was frantic, but it was too late."

"We are just human, you and me. But I want you to be free. Do it for yourself."

"Yes," she said. "We can start over, can't we?"

Chapter 17

Ethan rose early and had his coffee as he watched the sun come up through the camper window. His world had brightened after his time with Anna. They had shared their innermost thoughts and fears, had faced them together, and it had helped.

It was time for him to square his shoulders and just do his work. He'd done something less than honorable for a moment, but he'd made amends. Who in life hadn't had such lapses of courage? And as far as the custodial job itself, it wasn't much, but he was surrounded daily by the words and thoughts of thousands. In his own way, he stood guard over them with the best. Why should he diminish that or be diminished by it?

He finished his coffee and headed for the library. The weather was damp and drizzly as he made his way through the park. He passed the merry-go-round and the pier where they had talked. People were an odd species, struggling with their pasts, making themselves unhappy, even those as intelligent as Anna. But it had taken courage on her part to confide in him something so painful as the accidental death of her brother, and he had no intention of treating it lightly.

***

With his early start, he'd finished the first floor by the time Anna arrived. She waved discreetly at him from the checkout desk as he headed downstairs for his morning break. The basement was dark and dank on the best of days, but particularly so that day because of the gloomy weather that had set in overnight. It smelled slightly of mold, and the overhead light fixture was cluttered with dead bugs. Early on, he'd made a feeble attempt to cheer the place up by hanging a painting he'd acquired at a thrift. In the end, it had served only to highlight a crack that had developed in the wall.

As he was straightening his desk, he spotted an old envelope that had worked its way to the back of a drawer. To his surprise, it was addressed to Clarence Belowe. The return was not clear, having succumbed to the dampness of the basement, but it appeared to be Hathaway Buildings, Inc., Main Street. He was familiar with the old building, which had since been converted into a mini-mall.

He opened the envelope, finding a yellowed copy of a deposit slip for Belowe for three thousand dollars. The date had long since faded and was unreadable. The image of Belowe floating beneath the pier flashed before him, and his stomach tightened. In that moment he wondered if Captain Armen should be told about the deposit slip. Morrigan had urged him to keep things quiet, but what was Clarence Belowe doing with a check from Hathaway in the first place? And it was for a generous sum, considering the modest salary Belowe had been drawing.

Unable to convince himself that there was no good reason to tell the captain, he tucked the deposit slip into his pocket and tossed the empty envelope back into its drawer. He would get the slip to Captain Armen. There was a chance it might be of some use. For himself, it was a stretch to see any connection, but it might be worth a trip to the old Hathaway premises to see what he could find out.

***

A last-minute spill on the stairwell delayed closing. By the time he'd finished cleaning up, everyone had departed. He decided to walk downtown and check out the Hathaway Building. Evenings alone in the camper could get long, in any case.

The Hathaway Building itself was as he'd remembered it, an older, red-brick structure that had been restored and converted into a shopping mall, with boutique shops on the first floor and a department store taking up the second level. Not quite sure where to begin, he decided to take the elevator, a cranky, creaky old cage—meant to lend nostalgia—to the second floor. As he stepped out into the department store, an older lady approached and asked if she could help him.

"Just browsing," he said.

"Please make yourself at home. We have nice sales on, if you are looking for a special gift."

"Thank you, no. Look, I used to know a guy who worked here, at least I think he did, and I've been trying to locate him."

She turned. "Oh? Who might that be?"

"I'm not sure I remember his name."

"Well, I've been here a while," she said, smiling. "Try me."

"Clarence or Claude, something like that."

"We had a Clarence who worked here for a short time."

"Yeah, that's it, Clarence."

"Clarence Belowe was the building super for a couple of years," she said. "He's moved on, I'm afraid."

"Great guy," Ethan said. "You don't know where he went by chance? I'd like to see him again."

"Excuse me, please," she said, turning. "I have a customer waiting." She paused and looked back at him. "Clarence didn't talk about his personal life. You might check with the human resources office. It's possible they have an address on file."

"The office?"

"Up," she said, pointing to the elevator. "Ask Beth, the secretary."

"Yeah, thanks. I will."

Ethan punched the elevator button and waited for the old cage to clank upward, then finally settle to a stop. He waited for the door for several moments and was about to panic when it creaked open. He could see an office at the end of a hallway and a secretary at a desk, busy on the phone. She looked up when he came in and motioned for him to have a seat.

When she'd finished her call, she pushed her hair back and said, "Do you have a return?"

"No, I'm looking for someone who used to work here. The lady downstairs suggested I check with your office. I understand that he was the building super here."

"Name, please?"

"Clarence Belowe."

"Clarence? Oh, yes, Clarence did work here for a while. What did you want to see him about?"

"We are old friends. We haven't been in touch for a long time, and I thought I might look him up. Do you happen to have his address?"

"Well," she said, "Clarence has been gone for some time. I can't be certain where he is currently living."

"It's no big deal. I just thought that as long as I was in town . . . but thank you anyway."

"Well," she said, "I'm really not supposed to give out that kind of personal information, but you did say you were friends?"

"Yes, that's correct."

"Hang on. Let me take a quick look." At the file cabinet, she flipped through the folders.

"I suppose he could still be in town. Oh, yes, here it is. This was the address where he was living when he left. It's 416 Beasley Street."

"And could you tell me where that is?"

"It's an apartment complex, actually. Beasley is just off Main, east of Main."

"Thank you," he said. "You've been very helpful."

He started for the elevator, then hesitated. "You wouldn't know where he went to work from here, would you?"

"No, I'm sorry. He never said. Clarence struck me as someone who moved around quite a bit, though. Frankly, I wondered if he wasn't having financial problems. He left so suddenly and without notice. There were these people who kept calling for him. I think they may have been a collection agency or something. They aren't supposed to do that, you know."

***

Ethan punched the button and waited for the elevator to creak downward. So, Clarence had money problems. Maybe he gambled, got in trouble with the wrong crowd. That might account for his sudden disappearance and ultimate demise.

Back on the ground floor, Ethan took a moment to glance around and found himself in the midst of more stores: Benson's Boutique, Discount Shoes, Hathaway's Used and Rare Books. Out on the street, it was still light, and Beasley was not that far away, so he decided to check out the address.

He found the apartment complex, a vanilla, three-story firetrap with postage-stamp balconies that drooped perilously off the side of the building. The cars parked out front on the street were a testament to the occupants' substandard wages.

At the front desk stooped an old guy with foggy glasses. A cigarette smoldered in an ashtray next to an empty coffee mug. He pushed his glasses back up on his nose and examined Ethan.

"I'm looking for Clarence Belowe," Ethan said. "Do you happen to know him?"

The old guy took a drag off the cigarette, then squashed it out in the ashtray. His hands were gnarled with arthritis, and his fingers were stained yellow with tobacco.

"Yeah, I know Clarence Belowe," he said.

"He left me eating a month's rent. You looking to get your money back? Good luck on that."

"Did he live here long?" Ethan asked.

"Long enough. He claimed to be a building super, wanted to exchange work for rent. Turns out the bastard was holding down the same job over at the Hathaway Building. Playing both ends against the middle, wasn't he."

"Do you know what happened to him, where he went?"

He shook his head and shrugged. "Man owes you money don't leave a forwarding address, does he?"

"No, I suppose not," Ethan said.

"I don't know where he is. You find him. Tell him come see me. I got something I'd like to give him."

Chapter 18

Friday came; Ethan was on his way out of the library when he passed the Genealogy Room and spotted Anna up front, talking to a small group of people. She caught his eye and signaled for him to come in.

"Ethan," she said, "I'd like for you to meet our new book club members."

"I didn't mean to disturb," he said.

"You're good. This isn't school, you know. Ethan, this is Dakota Chance, our newest member. He's a philosophy student from the university. Dakota, this is Ethan, our library custodian."

Dakota nodded, and his earring, a single, large, silver orb, turned under the light.

"And you know Mia, I believe," Anna said.

Mia smiled, a full, warm smile, and wove her fingers in front of her. She wore a white, lacy blouse and denim shorts that gave away her youth.

"Hello, Ethan," she said.

"Mia."

"And over here is Imani Bell," Anna said, motioning to a large-boned, ebony-skinned woman. Imani turned her dark eyes on him. "Maybe you can help us with Diego, who we are hoping will make his book selection before the year passes."

Diego pointed his chin at Imani. "It will be a very big book."

Anna said, "And you've met Doris as well, the lady who has read more than the rest of us put together."

Doris was at the end of the table, clearly dated, what with her silver hair and flame-red lipstick. She had a large, cloth bag to her left and a leather purse of equal import to her right.

"You should join us, Ethan," she said. "We have a lovely leader."

"I would agree with that," Ethan said. "But someone must clean up around here. That's my territory."

Anna followed him to the door. "Maybe I'll see you later. We should be done around seven."

"I'll wait for you," he said, ducking out.

***

After he'd finished cleaning the library offices, Ethan waited at his shop desk for Anna to finish her meeting. Opening the desk drawer, he withdrew again the envelope with Clarence's name on it. What puzzled him was not the deposit slip's existence but its amount. It clearly exceeded what one would expect even in a monthly check. Perhaps it was not salary at all. Maybe Belowe had sold something of value to Hathaway. But what would a guy in a financial pinch have to sell for that kind of money?

Just then, Anna stuck her head in the doorway. "You're still here," she said.

He smiled, pointed to the chair. "Have a seat."

She sat down, crossed her legs, and sighed. "So, what did you think of the book club?"

"Quite an assortment, but they struck me as enthusiastic."

"Yes, though I did wonder about Diego and Dakota a bit."

"You mean Mia?"

"How did you know?"

"Male intuition."

"Are you suggesting that males *have* intuition?"

"Not exactly intuition so much as competition. She *is* attractive, you know."

"Oh, so you noticed too, did you?"

"Though not as attractive as the facilitator."

She looked at him. "Nice maneuver, Ethan. Really, I don't know how you men live with yourselves."

"That's why we love women so much. We don't have to."

She smiled and leaned forward, her eyes snapping, and he was reminded of just how pretty she really was.

"And so, about this Belowe thing," she said. "Have you heard more?"

Ethan shrugged. "Nothing more from Captain Armen. But . . . well, I did a little snooping on my own, actually. I worry that Belowe's death is not getting the attention it should. I did find some things of interest."

"Like?"

"Like, were you aware that Belowe had worked as building supervisor at the Hathaway mini-mall before he came to the library?"

Anna lay a finger on her lips. "I had no idea."

"And he was pulling double duty at his apartment complex."

"Then why the job here at the library? The money wouldn't be as good, I'm sure. Sorry, I didn't intend to demean your job. You are a bit sensitive about it, you know."

"The apartment manager implied that Belowe was less than forthright about things, that he left owing him money, in fact."

"I never saw that side of Clarence here at the library," she said. "He kept to himself. Did his work."

"It was suggested that something was going on with him financially."

"There was no indication, but he wasn't here long. He was a reticent kind of guy, so I actually knew little about him."

"From two building supers to janitor is a pretty steep drop in money for sure," he said. "The thing is, none of it spells winding up in a lake with a bullet hole in your back. Of course, money, or even the lack of it, can make a person susceptible to manipulation. There can be pressure, you know. Maybe he was a gambler, an addict or something?"

"It's possible, I suppose," she said. "To me, he was just an old guy doing a hard job."

"You would have thought that Morrigan would have checked him out before he hired him."

"Did he check you out?" she asked.

"Good point. Maybe he figures the job

doesn't require much in the way of character. I hope that's all Clarence Belowe and I have in common."

She looked at him. "What does that mean?"

"I wouldn't want to wind up like him."

"That isn't funny, Ethan."

"No, I suppose not. There's just something that doesn't add up here. This guy was quiet, right? Kept to himself? There was no indication that he was in some kind of trouble, broke maybe, and then he just disappears. Why would anyone bother to steal from an old guy who doesn't have anything to start with, much less kill him? What was worth taking that kind of risk?"

"It could have been random," she said. "Its been known to happen, Ethan. And sometimes people just find themselves in situations they hadn't anticipated, sometimes too late. I mean, you never expected to find a body floating in the lake, but it happened.

"Look, we can't really know what he was mixed up in, if anything. You should let this Belowe thing go. It's not really your job or mine. We probably will never know what happened to Clarence Belowe."

He looked at her and smiled. "You are not only smart, and pretty, but wise as well."

She smiled back and stood. "I should leave on that. Thanks for listening."

"I think you managed the club and Diego with considerable skill, Anna, while I, on the other hand, have completely failed in even preventing him from smoking in the furnace room."

"Diego is a lot smarter than we give him credit for, but you have to be looking for it. Perhaps your intuition only works with pretty women. Good night, Ethan."

Chapter 19

Anna's bungalow was small but cozy, complete with carefully matched furniture, a brimming bookcase, and a full array of family photographs. Anna fixed herself a glass of wine and browsed her book titles. They were eclectic and thoughtfully chosen. Though they were of little value in the rare book world, they served her purposes, and she cherished them for their content. Some she had read many times.

On the top shelf were the family photographs, including a small boy with dark hair and a crooked smile. Behind him stood a man, tall and stoic, and at his side a woman with flame-red hair, her chin lifted with curiosity.

She thought about her day and the book club with its array of personalities. While they had little in common in terms of culture, age, even lifestyle, the one thing the book club members shared was the need to explore their world. Spending time with a group so different, yet so driven in the same manner, was turning out to be special for her. She was beginning to think that this club thing was going to be one of the best parts of her job at the library.

She couldn't help but worry about Ethan and his situation with Captain Armen. While she didn't doubt his innocence in the whole thing, it could still complicate his life, maybe even endanger his job at the library. She didn't want that to happen. Maybe tomorrow she'd do a little checking on things herself. She could do it more easily and with less attracted attention than Ethan could. Although she couldn't be completely certain, she suspected that he was being watched a lot more closely by the authorities than he knew.

Anna fixed herself breakfast and watched the Sunday morning news. Her thoughts of Ethan lingered. To be honest with herself, she was drawn to him both emotionally and physically. She thought he felt the same way, but she couldn't be certain. He was a private sort of guy and not easily read, even though she'd sent out some pretty strong signals about her feelings. There was something about Ethan that she couldn't explain, as if he'd been damaged somehow along the line. Though he was endearing most of the time, he could also be distant. She didn't want to alarm him, so she told herself to take it slowly.

***

The day was sunny and bright as she struck out for a morning walk—something she savored and did routinely. Walking was a time beyond the reach of others, a time to think freely. It lifted her spirits and nourished the parsing of decisions. The solitude and exercise it provided were an antidote to the deadlines and crises that came up in the course of being alive. It was for her necessary, especially now that her feelings were so mixed. The alone time lifted her and freed her mind.

It was not by accident that she changed her usual route and found herself standing in front of the Hathaway Building, where Ethan had mentioned that Clarence Belowe had worked as a super. She'd been to the mall before and had found it to contain the usual lineup of department stores and boutiques.

She ducked into the small Hathaway Coffee Shop, ordered herself a cup, and settled back with a magazine that had been left on the table. She'd about decided that snooping into

Ethan's business was a bad idea when a young girl appeared at the register. It took a moment for her to recognize her as Mia Layla, the girl who had joined the book club. Not wanting to engage, Anna moved to a back booth and turned to her magazine.

Moments later, Dakota Chance came through the door, placed his order, and joined Mia at her table. Their greeting was one of old friends as they engaged in a lively chat. Anna had assumed that they had met at the book club but now wondered if she'd been wrong. Their conversation appeared warm and reciprocal. Having no desire to complicate matters with an accidental meeting, she waited for the right moment before slipping away.

On her way out, she noticed a sign, "Hathaway's Used and Rare Books." She'd heard of the store but had never been in. At some point, she would return and visit, when there were fewer distractions. Browsing in a bookstore was a busman's holiday, she supposed, but it was still something she enjoyed doing.

She passed the library on her walk back and found the parking lot empty, it being a Sunday morning. In the absence of people, birds had cheerfully gathered there for their morning social. She started homeward, paused, then turned back to face the library. What drew her to do so was not clear to her—curiosity, she supposed. Whatever the motivation, she needed to know.

Unlocking the back door, she shut off the security alarm and made her way to the checkout area. Sunlight, mollified through the stained glass, seeped quietly and gently down from the rotunda. In the absence of people, the library was crypt-like in its silence, filled only with books and words. Though libraries were considered to be quiet spaces, just the opposite had been her experience. The daily voices were most often hushed, but the search and hum and movement of people were constant. This was Sunday, though, and the one day during the week on which the library was empty.

Even so, there was a presence in those chambers, in those thousands of tomes where the secrets existed, the power to change and stir the imagination in the most profound ways, to offer up knowledge, love, and terror. For her to be alone in their presence this way was both satisfying and eerie.

She brought up the library card records on the computer and typed in Mia Layla's name. Her address came up as 4510 East Oak Street, and her employment was listed as sales clerk, Hathaway Women's Clothes. Then she entered Dakota Chance's name but found nothing.

Sitting back, she wondered at Dakota's lack of a library card. How odd that a young guy like him had joined a book club but had never even applied for a card. Of course, there was Mia's allure, which might easily have reeled him in.

She rose and went to the stairwell, turned on the light, then turned it off again. There was really no reason for her to go there. Why was she drawn to his workplace? She hesitated, flipped on the light, and made her way down the stairs. She was, after all, the librarian and had every right to be there. No one could legitimately question her checking it out. It was really a matter of making certain that all was well. After all they'd been through with the custodial situation, she needed to keep an eye on things.

Ethan's desk was cleared and ordered, as she'd suspected it would be, and the room smelled slightly of his cologne. She sat in his chair and thought about the conversations they'd had. She opened the desk drawer and looked through its contents. She shouldn't have. It was crazy adolescent, she knew. But she wondered how he spent his time alone down there.

At the back of the drawer, she found an empty envelope with Clarence Belowe's name on it. The smudged return address read Hathaway Buildings, Inc. This must be how Ethan traced Belowe to his previous employment location, she thought. She put it back in the drawer. She wished the whole incident would just go away. It had complicated what could have been a comfortable progression in their relationship.

She had just closed the desk drawer when she heard something, a door perhaps, footsteps in the stairwell. She looked around for a place to hide. The furnace room door was ajar, so she slipped in and pulled the door closed.

Darkness, the stale smell of heat and tobacco smoke, enveloped her. A shaft of light suddenly lit from under the furnace room door, then went off as quickly. She held her breath in the darkness. She could hear footsteps making their way back up the stairwell, then they were gone. She waited in the darkness to make certain that all was silent, and then waited more, because this was not the place she wanted to be found, not by Morrigan, or Ethan, or anyone else.

Chapter 20

Mia Layla and Dakota Chance didn't show up at the next book club meeting. All the while, Diego stood in the back with his hat on and a book under his arm. Having waited as long as she could, Anna said, "Mr. Diego Pinto has been selecting our first book to read. Have you made a decision yet, Diego?"

Taking his hat off, Diego stepped forward and held up the book. "I have made the decision. It is a very good book, and all here should read it right away."

Anna looked around the room. Everyone was intent on hearing what Diego had selected. "Well, tell us the title and the name of the author please, Diego."

"The title of my book is *All They Will Call You,* and it is written by Mr. Tim Hernandez."

"And is this a book that we all can read and enjoy?"

Diego looked around the room at the others. "This is a very good book," he said. "Very big."

"And you will be prepared to lead our discussion at our next meeting, won't you?" Anna asked.

"I will lead on about this book because I have led such a life as this. I will know all the answers, you will see."

"That's fine, Diego," she said. "I'll make certain that we have copies available in the library for those who wish to check one out. Now, since we have two members absent, and we have yet to read our first selection, I'm going to dismiss the group. Does anyone have questions?"

Doris, the older lady, said, "Is this book in English?"

Anna looked at Diego. "English, Diego?"

"*Sí,*" he said. "For those who can speak only one language."

"Yes, well . . . ," Anna said, "so this week we will all read Diego's selection. Please be prepared to ask questions that you might have for him, or points that you would like to explore at our next meeting. Until then, happy reading."

Diego waited until after everyone had gone before approaching Anna. "Is there something I could help you with, Diego?" she asked.

"Do you think my book is a good book?"

"Well, I haven't read it yet, but if it's important

to you, that's enough." Diego held the book to his chest and looked around. "Was there something else, Diego?"

"Some of the people were not here tonight. I think maybe they quit because immigrants should not be in such a public way."

"No one has quit as far as I know, Diego, and you have a perfect right to be in the club."

"Maybe Mia and the man with the earring. They are not here tonight."

"I've not been contacted by either of them, Diego, but no one is required to attend the meetings. In any case, I don't think you need to be concerned. I'm sure it has nothing to do with you."

"Oh, I do not worry," he said, looking down at his feet. "Maybe they ran away together. The man thinks of nothing but Mia."

Anna closed her notebook and leaned back in her chair. "Perhaps you are thinking about Mia a lot too, Diego."

Diego shook his head. "I don't see the way Mia walks, but the man sees."

"What do you mean?"

"The way she moves, like in a song, I think."

"Mia moves like in a song?"

"It's not for me to notice. If something should happen to Mia, they would come for me, an immigrant. The man is not good for Mia, I think. Maybe they have run away?"

"Well, that's beyond the purview of a book club facilitator, Diego. Club members' private lives are private."

"You will tell Mia that I have selected an important book, that she should attend and hear my talk?"

"If I see her. And you *will* be ready, won't you?"

He walked to the door. "Don't worry, Anna. I will be ready." He hesitated. "Ethan is in the basement. I think he wants to join the book club, but he is afraid. Maybe you should talk to him."

***

Anna found Ethan at his desk in the basement doing paperwork. "Hi," she said.

He looked up and smiled. "You're finished so soon?"

"Small group tonight," she said. "Diego thought I should come down and put pressure on you to join the club. He thinks you are afraid."

"That's it," Ethan said. "Diego has a way of owning the room. I'm not sure I could compete."

"Well, yes, Diego is an acquired taste,

but memorable, you must admit. Are you OK, Ethan? I have the feeling that you've been avoiding me."

"All this time, I thought you were avoiding me. It's nothing to do with you, Anna. It's just that I needed to do some catching up. My life has gotten pretty complicated lately."

"Ethan, I don't mean to interfere, but please tell me if—"

"Oh, no, you aren't interfering. It's nothing like that, Anna. I suppose it's this Belowe thing hanging over me. I thought it was over, you know."

"What's wrong? What's going on?"

"Captain shows up at my camper last night. He had tracked Clarence Belowe to the Hathaway Building and was told that I had been there ahead of him." Ethan pushed his chair back and rubbed at his face. "I had given him a deposit slip of Belowe's that I found in the shop desk. He'd checked Belowe's banking records and confirmed that he had made several large deposits. He said that Belowe's deposits were too large for a man on a custodian's salary, that maybe he was involved in some sort of drug activity. He questioned me for some time about what I was doing at the Hathaway Building. I got the feeling that he thought I was interfering with the investigation."

"He's just fishing for information."

"Maybe, but it's uncomfortable."

Anna crossed her arms and pursed her lips. "OK, so I have a confession to make."

"Oh?"

"I went to the Hathaway Building myself the other day, just curious after what you told me. So, anyway, I stopped in for a coffee at the shop there, and guess who comes in?"

"Who?"

"Mia Layla and Dakota Chance."

"What were they doing there?"

"They were having a lively conversation. I didn't want to be seen, so I slipped out. But an odd thing . . ."

"What?"

"They didn't show up for the club meeting tonight. It struck me as peculiar that neither came."

"Maybe they are just getting together, a romantic relationship or something. It's been known to happen."

"Yes, I suppose it's possible. And it is a public coffee shop. I thought of that, of course, and Mia had worked in the building at some point, but still . . . I mean, first Clarence and then them. It's probably nothing, but both connected to the Hathaway and to the library. It's just odd, isn't it?"

"In the same mall where Clarence worked as a building super," he said.

"Well," she said, standing, "I should get home. May I give you a ride?"

"Thanks, Anna, but I've some catching up to do. Morrigan failed to tell me that ordering supplies was part of my job description."

She picked up her things. "You are welcome to join the club, you know. We'd love to have you, and I think you could compete with Diego quite well, actually."

"Thank you, Anna. Maybe when things have leveled out. I'll see you tomorrow."

Chapter 21

When Ethan awoke the next morning, he dressed and fixed a quick breakfast before heading out. The morning was misty, and the clouds were dark with rain as they drifted over the park lake.

He thought once to stop at the pier, but he'd slept late, and Morrigan was a stickler about opening at the exact proper moment. The one thing the custodial job had going for it was its predictability. Today's duties would be exactly like yesterday's and every other day's. While the tedium of the work made it bearable, it also made it difficult. The absence of human interaction made it tolerable, but lonely.

Clarence Belowe must have experienced the same feelings about the work. Even though they had never met, there was a connection between them—the same job, the same isolation, the same indifference from others. Although people at times acknowledged

Ethan's presence, it was perfunctory for the most part and clear they did not fully see him.

So who was Belowe, really? Where did he come from? What brought him to such an ignoble end? There had to be tracks in the sand, records somewhere of his uncelebrated life. Ethan thought about the details Anna had so easily uncovered from no more than a library card. He wondered if maybe some of Clarence Belowe's past might be on file as well.

***

He waited until the lunch break to catch Anna coming out of her office. Her hair was swept back in a copper spill, and her turquoise eyes sparkled. She smiled when she saw him.

"Listen," he said, "I've been thinking, about this Clarence Belowe business. There's so much not known about him."

"What are you getting at, Ethan?"

"We don't really even know who he was. I was thinking that his job application might still be on file here at the library."

She spiked her hands on her waist and squinted her eyes at him. "Ethan Poser, are you asking me to steal Clarence Belowe's file?"

"Not steal, just look."

"Really, I could get fired for something like that."

"It's an employment application," he said. "Who would even know?"

She took hold of his arm. "Not so loud, or everyone will know. Anyway, people lie on those things all the time. You probably did."

"Me? Never."

She rolled her eyes. "Let me do some checking."

"You're the best, Anna."

"The dumbest, you mean. Where?"

"Hathaway Coffee Shop after work."

"OK, but if I get in trouble . . ."

"See you there."

***

He was waiting when Anna arrived at the coffee shop with a folder in one hand and her purse in the other.

"An odd choice for a meeting place," she said.

"Did you bring it?"

She handed him the folder. "I risked my life for you. I need to get that folder back."

After reading through it, he said, "There's not much here. I was hoping for more."

"Nothing about his financial problems?" she asked. "Funny Belowe forgot that. But there is one thing."

"Oh?"

She flipped back a page. "Here they ask to list a person to contact in case of an emergency. A Sissy Bluestone, 202 Burnham Street, and there's a phone number too."

"But who is Sissy Bluestone? His wife, maybe, or an ex?"

"Belowe indicated that he was single. It could be anyone—mother, girlfriend. Who knows?"

"Maybe we could call?"

"Look, buster, you've already implicated me in a theft. I had to break into Morrigan's locked file cabinet for this."

He took her hand. "Thanks, Anna. I won't forget it."

"Are you sure you shouldn't leave this business to the police, Ethan?"

"As soon as they leave *me* out of it, I'll reconsider."

He watched as she left, catching another glimpse of her as she went by the window and out onto the street. She was a beauty, and game too. He liked her a lot. After she'd gone, he opened his phone and dialed Sissy Bluestone's number.

"Hello," a woman said.

"Ms. Bluestone? Sissy Bluestone?"

"Yes, this is she."

"My name is Ethan Poser. I'm an employee at the Carnegie Library. Your name and number were listed as a contact for a Mr. Clarence Belowe."

"Clarence? Yes, I know Clarence. What is it?"

"Something has come up. Do you mind if we meet? This is not an issue that can be easily handled over the telephone."

"Carnegie Library, you say?"

"That's correct. It wouldn't take long. We could meet at Hathaway Coffee Shop, if you prefer."

"Well, I'm just home from work."

"Are you still on Burnham Street?"

"Yes."

"That's not far from here. I could be there in a few minutes."

"Well, I suppose that would be OK," she said. "I do have plans later."

"Thank you, Ms. Bluestone. I'll see you shortly."

He hung up. It was a long shot, but he

had a hunch that Captain Armen had not been down this path yet. And he had to admit to a certain exhilaration at being ahead of the game.

***

The house was a bungalow with a screened-in porch that had succumbed to an overgrown lilac bush. An older-model car sat in the driveway, a Chevy coupe with smooth front tires.

He rang the doorbell and waited. A woman opened the door a crack. Her hair was graying, and her lipstick had migrated into the lines of her mouth.

"Ms. Bluestone?" he asked.

"Yes. Are you the one who called?"

"I'm sorry to bother you, Ms. Bluestone, but I have some news."

"About Clarence?" she asked.

"May I come in?"

"Oh, yes, come in." She opened the door and pointed to the couch. "Please excuse the house. I'm just home, you see. Is Clarence in some sort of trouble?"

"He listed you as an emergency contact, Ms. Bluestone. It doesn't say what your connection is. Are you related?"

She shook her head. "Oh, no, we were friends for a while—close friends, actually. Has something happened to Clarence?"

"I'm afraid so, Ms. Bluestone. You see, his body was recovered from the park lake. He'd been shot."

"Oh, my," she said, her eyes filling.

"We've been trying to track down relatives and thought you might be of some help."

She sat down and folded her hands in her lap. "Clarence, dead?"

"Do you know if there are people who should be notified, family, that sort of thing?"

She shook her head. "He told me he had no one left. That's probably why he put my name down as a contact. So sad. But it's not entirely unexpected."

"Oh?"

"I sometimes wondered if things might not catch up with Clarence."

"I don't understand."

"At first he seemed like such an ordinary fellow, a guy who went to work every day, like that, you know. But then I started finding out things."

"What do you mean?"

"For example, he'd been incarcerated, in Canada, actually. He was from there, Nova

Scotia, I think it was. He said he did time in Springhill correctional facility there for receiving stolen property. He said it was all a mistake."

"Did you believe him?"

"At first, but you learn a person over time, don't you? Clarence was always looking for a way to ingratiate himself."

"To you as well?"

She nodded. "First he broke my heart, and then on the way out, he took what little money I had. It's hard to forgive that, isn't it?"

"Do you know of anyone who would want to kill him?"

She rubbed at her arms. "Clarence didn't care much about anyone, not in any real way. I suppose there were those who might have wanted revenge."

Ethan stood to leave. "I'm sorry, Ms. Bluestone. Thank you for the information."

"Do you know where he is now?" she asked. "His body, I mean."

He thought for a moment. "A public health burial is provided when there is no one to claim a body. Is there something you want to do for him?"

"No," she said, shaking her head. "Nothing."

Chapter 22

Anna returned Belowe's job application to the file cabinet first thing the next morning. Although the personnel files were under lock in Morrigan's office, she'd been issued a key, which she rarely used. All of the other facility keys and the book collection records were kept in the file cabinet as well. Morrigan was careful not to discuss book prices or trade negotiations with anyone, maintaining that publicizing such information only jeopardized any purchasing advantages that the foundation might have.

Over the next few days, she used what spare time she could manage to read Diego's book, making notes and constructing questions for the upcoming meeting. Diego's selection was well thought out and fitting. She'd gotten the distinct feeling that Diego did not read books on a regular basis—at least, that had been her observation in the library. The book dealt with some rather sensitive immigration issues that were still current today, and she hoped he'd not gotten himself in too deep.

The night of the club meeting, she checked the stairwell to see if Ethan might have stayed over for the session, but his office was dark. She'd thought he might have reconsidered joining the book club. But she understood that he was disturbed with Captain Armen's intimations about his connection to Belowe's death. It was not the best time to press him about joining the club.

In the Genealogy Room, Anna greeted two new members: Van Number, an old bachelor who worked as a bank cashier, an amiable sort who was always willing to engage in small talk, and another recruit by the name of Sophia Abel. Anna was somewhat familiar with her as a regular patron of the library. She often came in looking for the most current romances. She struck Anna as a lonely person, one who rarely shared anything personal. It was only through the grapevine that Anna had learned of the death of Sophia's husband, a tragic car accident that had cut his life short several years past.

The other members had gathered in the meeting room, including Doris, who had brought cheesecake and coffee for a post-meeting treat. Everyone took their seats in anticipation of Diego's discussion. After Anna had introduced the two new members, she turned to Diego, who typically preferred the back row but now sat front and center. He had abandoned his usual hat and denims for a dress shirt and slacks.

"My, Diego," Anna said, "don't you look nice tonight."

"*Gracias,*" he said. "I wore this last at my mother's funeral. It is all right?"

"Very appropriate," she said. "So, are you ready to share your book with the group?"

"I share this with them now," he said.

"Did you not make notes, Diego?"

"It's better to come from the heart," he said.

"Yes, absolutely." She motioned for Diego to come up to the podium. "The floor is yours, Diego."

He stood with shoulders squared, took a deep breath, and began. "This book is about my people," he said. "It tells how hard they work and how much they love their families. It tells about how they came to El Norte to pick the fruit and vegetables so they could send a little money home to their loved ones. It tells how they died in a plane crash as they were being deported back to Mexico.

"I like this book because it reminds me that these were people who were loved and should not be remembered only as immigrants, as strangers, but as husbands and wives, brothers and sisters.

"You must think how hard to be an immigrant. You say we are here to take your jobs. This is true. We take the jobs who all will not take. It is too hard to pick the green beans until the arms bleed or to stand high on the ladder to pick the fruit from the trees, or to sleep sometimes on the ground or in the huts with so many men who cry out in the night for home.

"You must think how we miss our families, and the beautiful *señorita* who awaits our return. Sometimes we were men of honor at home, who had jobs and pride, and now we are men who only wait for hope. Everything we were, we are no more, and we are here only to work. There is so much to us is strange. The language is so hard, and we do not hear the beat of the *mariachi* or taste the flavors of our food.

"Sometimes I see it in the eyes of the American, and I know what it is. Please do not look *at* me but look *into* me, and know what is true."

Diego went on to the tell the stories of each of the victims of the terrible crash of an airplane carrying deported immigrants back to Mexico. Tears came into his eyes as he brought their stories to life. The club members, at first skeptical, were soon taken by Diego's words, by their sadness and loneliness and sincerity. Only he could have related the material with such authenticity.

Anna's throat tightened with emotion as she listened to him describe how these people, his people, had been lost to obscurity so long ago. And she knew that he spoke not only of their plight and the pain of their families but of his own.

Diego was a man who himself had been asked too often to step aside because of who he was, or, more accurately, because of who he wasn't. And when he'd finished his talk, the room fell silent, and then a question, and then another, and then an outpouring.

Diego had won them with his truth. Anna promised herself never again to assume what a person was until she'd known their heart. It was there to be found, or not, in their character.

When he'd taken his seat, the members of

the club applauded, and Diego smiled broadly. Not only had he made a perfect book selection but he had transformed it into a real and personal experience that no one but he could have done.

Anna dismissed the meeting, and when the members had had their fill of cheesecake, they drifted away, until only Diego and Anna remained.

"It was OK, Anna?" he asked.

"It wasn't OK, Diego. It was marvelous."

His smile widened. "I have known always that this was a good place for me," he said. "I come with my poor English and my poor education, and everyone smiles with me. I come here to be among the books and my friends, just like everyone."

***

Anna had shut out the lights and was on her way to closing when she paused at the computer. On impulse, she typed in Diego Pinto's name. He had indeed acquired a library card days earlier and had checked out *All They Will Call You.* He'd also acquired a recording of the book made available from the library by the League for the Blind.

Chapter 23

Ethan debated whether to contact Anna. It was the weekend, and already the camper was pressing in on him. He could take her out for breakfast or a walk. They'd had little enough time to discuss things. Truth was, he missed being with her.

He picked up his phone and dialed her number.

"Hello," she said, a bit breathless.

"Anna, this is Ethan. I didn't wake you?"

"Ha!" she said. "I've been exercising for hours. What's going on?"

"Was hoping we might get together, maybe coffee or something?"

"Are you buying?"

"Of course. Money is nothing to me."

"Uh-huh. How about Hathaway Coffee Shop? I'm in the vicinity. I'll meet you there."

"Works for me," he said. "See you in a bit."

***

Anna was waiting for him on the bench just outside the entrance when he got there. She was wearing white shorts and a black T and had her hair tied back with a bandanna. Her face was rosy with exercise.

"Morning," he said, dropping down beside her. "I didn't know you were a runner."

"Running doesn't quite describe it, Ethan. It's more like coasting."

"So, I'm buying," he said. "Lead the way."

She took his arm as they went into the coffee shop. He could feel the heat of her against him and the soft dampness of her hand on his arm.

He bought her coffee and slid into the booth next to her. "I must say, you look stunning this morning, Anna. I didn't realize you had this athletic side."

"Just stop, Ethan. A walk to the coffee shop does not constitute athletic prowess."

The coffee smelled dark roasted and rich, and he took a sip. "So, tell me about the book club meeting."

Her face lit, and she laughed, more of a chortle, the sound one might make when given good news. "You won't believe it, Ethan. Diego was marvelous. He had the whole group mesmerized before he was finished."

"This is the same Diego who sleeps in the reference section and smokes cigarettes in the furnace room?"

"His book was about these Mexican immigrants in the forties who were being deported from the US on an airplane. It crashed near the border, and they were killed. They never made it home, and the families were left to wonder what had happened to them. Diego teared up when he told the story, and we did as well. It was very moving."

"I'm pleased, Anna. I admit to having been a little skeptical."

"And here's the astonishing thing. He did the entire presentation from memory, not a single note."

Ethan looked up from his cup. "That's pretty incredible."

Anna set her cup aside and leaned in. "So, I took the liberty of looking him up on the library computer, and guess what?"

"What?"

"The only thing he has ever checked out from the library is an audio recording of that same book."

"A recording?"

"I'm telling you, I don't think Diego can

read. He'd committed the whole thing to memory, and then he answered every question the group posed. His command of the details was quite remarkable."

"I do say, I'm impressed."

"But you can never say anything to him, Ethan. Never."

"I had planned on giving him a bit of a stir about it."

"If you bring it up, I will get even with you. I promise."

He looked at her over his cup. "Just remember that I have considerable inside information about a recent larceny that took place in Morrigan's office. I could choose to use it, if necessary."

"Not if your legs are broken."

They finished their coffee and went out into the entryway. "By the by," he said, "I called Sissy Bluestone."

"Clarence Belowe's emergency contact?"

"The same. In fact, I went to see her. Turns out she isn't a relative but an ex-girlfriend of his. She told me that Clarence Belowe was a bit of a con artist, that he had done time in the Springhill correctional facility in Nova Scotia."

She looked up through her brows. "Prison?

Belowe? I would never have thought such a thing."

"Receiving stolen goods. She said his modus operandi was to work his way into the good graces of people, gain their trust, and then take advantage. She said he was good at it."

"And that's what he did to her?"

"Sounded like it to me. One wonders how he wound up taking a job at the library."

"And who might have caught up with him there?"

"I kept thinking maybe the whole business was just coincidental, but then I remember Captain Armen saying that there is no such thing as coincidence."

"We will never know why he was killed, I guess."

"Or does anyone actually care? To date, the investigation has not been that aggressive. Captain Armen has even failed to track down Belowe's old prison record, far as I know."

When they'd stepped out onto the sidewalk, he said, "How about a lift home?"

"I'm not ready for the day to be over. Hey, why don't we go to that bookstore here in the mall? I hear it's really nice."

"Busman's holiday?" he said, taking her hand.

"I know, but still . . ."

"Come on, then. We'll go look at books."

The bookstore was brightly painted with a huge "Used and Rare Books" painted on the front window.

"I love these places," she said.

"You spend forty hours a week surrounded by books, Anna."

"Not enough. Besides, Dr. Morrigan keeps the fun stuff locked away."

The store was floor to ceiling books, all with the warmth and smell of aging paper and leather. Two clerks sat at the front with their morning coffee. In the back, a room with a front-facing observation window had been constructed. A middle-aged man, wearing white gloves and enormous tortoiseshell glasses, was getting a book from one of the shelves. He brought the volume forward, opened it on the table, and laid a card beside it.

"Oh, look," Anna said, "he's set out one of their rare books. Let's see."

Anna trailed her fingers over the titles as they made their way through the shelves to the back of the store. Instructions posted on the collection's door stated the procedure for requesting a title to be examined. The man with the glasses had disappeared back into the stacks.

Anna leaned in to read the card through the window. "It's an autographed 1940 first edition of *For Whom the Bell Tolls* by Ernest Hemingway," she said. "It says it's signed, in 'very good' condition with a slight tear on the dust jacket corner. Oh my gosh, the price is seven thousand dollars."

Anna cupped her eyes with her hands against the window and studied the book. "A first-edition Hemingway," she said to herself.

"Rare, I'm assuming," he said.

She looked over at him and lifted her brows. "Rare indeed, though the 'very good' condition diminishes its value to some degree."

"Well, it's a bit out of my price range or I'd pick up a copy for you," he said.

A bald man with a briefcase approached from the front, knocked on the door next to them, and waited. The man with the tortoiseshell glasses came from out of the stacks and unlocked the door. He offered the man a seat at the table, where he examined the book for several minutes before a discussion commenced between them.

Anna took Ethan's arm. "Come on. I should get back."

Anna was quiet as they made their way to the car. She opened the door and said, "You know, one of our new club members, Sophia Abel, said she was joining the club but that she had wanted to select her own books instead of letting someone else do it. I hope I've organized that club well."

"Some folks follow a narrow path, Anna. I wouldn't worry about it. Isn't there something more you'd like to do today?"

"I should get home," she said. "I have to read Doris's book selection and make a few notes before our next meeting. I do so want this club to work, you know."

The day had warmed, and the streets were empty as they drove back to Anna's house. After pulling in to her driveway, he shut off the engine. Anna sat quietly for a moment, looking out the window.

"Anna," he said, "are you OK?"

She glanced over at him. "I was just thinking about that book we saw in the rare book room."

"The Hemingway?"

She nodded. "I had this moment."

"I could tell," he said. "What's that all about, Anna?"

"I'm not sure I know. It was a feeling."

"Well, it's not every day you get to see a 1940, signed, first edition of *For Whom the Bell Tolls*. It *was* pretty remarkable."

"Yes," she said. "But it was more than just seeing it."

"What do you mean?"

"I read everything by Hemingway in college, you know. I was completely taken with his work when I was younger. Me and everyone else in the country, I suppose." Her eyes glistened with tears, and she touched them away. "When I saw that book, knowing that it was a first edition, and with Hemingway's actual signature, I was completely swept away for a moment."

"It's a rare book, Anna. We don't get to see many of them."

"I know, and it was quite visceral for me. I've never been a collector, but I've seen a good number of them come through the library. I could never quite understand their passion until now. For the briefest moment, I wanted that book with everything that was in me."

"There are plenty of Hemingway books in our library, Anna."

"I know, but not that one. I wanted to *own* that one. I wanted it for myself. It was quite the strangest feeling." She turned and looked at him. "It was like knowing that someone special to you has died and then to suddenly see them alive. That's what it felt like, like a miracle had just taken place."

"Well, collectors are a strange lot," he said. "That I know. I once had a friend who collected tigereye agate shooters."

"What's that?"

"Marbles. I mean, no kidding, he collected these things. There wasn't anything he wouldn't do to get one for his collection."

"Marbles?"

"Yep. He had hundreds of them. He talked about them all the time, like they were gold or something, you know, and yet I never met another person who collected them. When he would get a new one, he'd bring it to school and show it to everyone. The thing is, the more he collected, the more he wanted. It was like an addiction."

"Divine, mystical sort of. Scary, like being out of control. There is a name for it in the book trade, actually."

"What's that?"

"Bibliomania," she said. "It's a good job I don't have money, Ethan, or I would be thousands short at this moment." She opened the door to get out and paused. "Did you ever feel that way?"

"Yes, about certain people," he said, smiling.

Chapter 24

Ethan took his lunch break in his shop. It gave him the opportunity to collect his thoughts and even take a short snooze if he felt like it. He'd been thinking a lot about Belowe and his life and the sequence of events associated with his death. He'd written them down in the hope of connecting some of the dots, but so far, everything seemed rather random and disconnected.

He was headed upstairs to the mezzanine to finish before quitting time when Diego came in.

"Hey, *amigo*," he said. "Maybe you brought a banana today?"

"It's in the sack, Diego."

Diego sported a white shirt and had trimmed his hair, which had grown long over his collar.

Peeling the banana, he said, "I hope the green banana doesn't give me the stomachache."

"Me too," Ethan said. "I wouldn't want you to stop eating my lunch every day. And

I suppose you have come to smoke up the shop as well."

"I have stopped smoking," he said.

"Excuse me?"

He took a bite of the banana. "A man of literature should not smoke."

Ethan looked at him. "I see. And so how did the book club meeting go?"

"A standing ovation. I have a way with words."

"I can't disagree there," Ethan said. "Now, I must get to work. Just make yourself at home, Diego."

"I, too, must get to work. I have many books to read. You should join the club, Ethan. Anna prefers men who are well read."

***

Ethan was on his way to the mezzanine when Anna motioned him over from the stacks. "I'd like to talk to you. Could we meet after work today?"

"Where?"

"At Hathaway Coffee Shop. I'm buying."

"I'll be there," he said.

The mezzanine was quiet and shadowy, as

several of the drapes had been drawn against the afternoon sunlight. Some of the less valuable books had been shelved outside the collections room. Even so, Morrigan kept the light to a minimum against the possibility of damaging them. According to Anna, dust jackets of age were especially prone to fading in bright conditions.

He'd nearly finished for the day and was gathering up his cleaning supplies when he felt a presence. He turned to find Dr. Morrigan standing in the shadows behind him.

"Oh, Dr. Morrigan," he said. "You startled me."

Morrigan stepped forward into the light. "I wonder if we might have a word?"

Ethan pushed his cleaning cart aside. "What is it?"

"It has been reported that people have been loitering on this floor. As you know, Special Collections is located here. Those volumes are irreplaceable and quite valuable. This area must remain secure at all times."

"I haven't seen anyone loitering," Ethan said. "But I'm not up here much of the day."

"The mezzanine area is not to be used for public gatherings. If you see anyone who doesn't belong, I want it reported."

"I could put a sign up if you want."

"Yes," he said, turning for the stairs, "a sign might help."

***

Anna was at the coffee shop when Ethan arrived. He settled into the booth with his coffee and watched as she put her glasses into her purse. Her hair had fallen down over an eye, and she pushed it aside with a finger.

"What?" she said.

"Just admiring. Did you know that your eyes are the color of seawater?"

"Just stop, Ethan. I already told you I would buy the coffee."

"Oh, yeah, I forgot. By the way, I had a visit from Diego today. He says that you prefer literary types, like him, I'm assuming, and that I should join the club or risk losing out."

"Well, I *am* drawn to that sort of man, I admit," she said, smiling. "And you should know that Diego has already checked out a recording of Doris's club selection. He takes it all quite seriously, unlike some people I know."

"You wanted to talk to me, Anna. What about?"

She stirred her coffee, set her spoon aside. "I kept thinking about that book we saw at the bookstore. I couldn't get it out of my head."

"The Hemingway?"

She nodded. "There was something about it that was so familiar, something beyond the author, title, and copyright date, or even the signature. And then it came to me."

"What did?"

"When I was newly hired for the library position, Dr. Morrigan conducted a tour of the facility, including Special Collections. It was one of the few times I've actually been in there for any length of time. The thing is, we were looking at the Hemingway collection when he pointed out their newly acquired copy of his 1940 first edition of *For Whom the Bell Tolls.* It was a signed copy too."

"Like the one in the bookstore?"

"Exactly."

"But there must be more copies available other places?" he said.

"I'm sure, but then I remembered something. Morrigan talked about condition and how even the slightest damage to a rare book can diminish its value."

"Like a dust jacket tear?"

"He pointed out a tear on that book's dust jacket, Ethan. I'm sure it was the same tear in the same place that was on that bookstore copy."

Ethan studied his coffee cup. "You think that the bookstore has the library's copy?"

"I can't be sure, but I'm pretty certain it's the same copy. It could have been a lawful transaction, I suppose. Morrigan could have traded up for something of more value. It's the only lawful way a book can be sold or traded."

"Or it could have been stolen from Special Collections?"

"Theoretically, I suppose so."

"How does one find out such things?"

"The easiest way would be to check the collection's appraisal records."

"And where would those be?"

"In Morrigan's office file. And if the book is still on the appraisal record, we would need to check the collection for the physical copy."

Ethan laid his finger alongside his nose and looked around. "We're going to break into the Special Collections room?"

"Technically, it isn't breaking in, not if you use the key."

"And where do we find this key? Because I don't think Morrigan's inclined to help."

"It's the spare key, and it's in the same file cabinet as the appraisals."

***

They waited until dark to enter through the back door of the library. Ethan shut off the alarm and held the door open for Anna. They stood for a moment to let their eyes adjust to the darkness. The library was quiet and still. He'd known that level of stillness only a few times in his life, and it usually had something to do with death. Then he heard Anna take a deep breath, and he rubbed the tension from his arms.

They made their way through the stacks to the central office, which was little more than a small cubicle with a large glass window. The cubicle reminded Ethan of a prison watch tower from which one had a panoramic view of the yard. No violation, no matter how small, could go unnoticed from there.

A computer was on the desk, its light on, a red eye in the darkness. The library, in all its emptiness, pressed in about them.

"So where is this file?" he asked.

She pointed. "Over there."

"Can we turn the light on?"

"I brought a flashlight," she said. "It's small, so you will have to hold it."

"Do you know what Morrigan would do to us if he found out we were in here?"

"He would do nothing to me," she said.

"Why's that?"

"Because I would swear that you kidnapped me, that you dragged me in here, and that I had no choice."

He clicked on the flashlight, which lit the office far more brightly than he'd expected.

"Shine it over here, Ethan."

"Where?"

"On the file cabinet, please. Really, Ethan, if you are going to be a burglar, you must pay attention."

"I was just thinking about the kidnapping. Did I tie you up?"

"Very funny," she said. Taking his hand, she directed the light onto the cabinet. She took a key from her pocket and unlocked it. After searching through a drawer, she brought out a small box of paper clips.

"Found it," she said.

"What?"

"The spare key to Special Collections."

"In a paper clip box?"

"Would you have found it?"

"It would have been the first place I'd have looked."

"Right. Here are the appraisal records. Hold the light there," she said, scanning the page.

"Is that an appraisal of the entire collection?"

"I'm sure," she said, flipping to the back page. "Here it is: twelve million, two hundred thousand."

"Did you say twelve million? How is that possible?"

"Benefactors, collectors mostly," she said. "Their collections represent a lifetime of research and negotiations from all over the world. There is nothing more important to them than keeping their collections secure and intact, and that includes after their deaths."

"But twelve million? We are talking books here, right?"

She opened another folder and extracted a paper. "Look at this one," she said. "At the time of this appraisal, the market value of *The Laws of the United States,* 1803, signed by Thomas Jefferson, was two hundred twenty-five thousand dollars. And then there's Newton's

Principia, nearly a million dollars alone. We have both of them right up there."

"I had no idea any book went for that kind of money. If I had a rare book, I wouldn't know what to do with it."

"Collectors are experts, Ethan. They study the rare book business like stockbrokers study the market. The truth is that rare book sales are not always legitimate. Stolen books are acquired all the time, and by people you wouldn't think. Even museums have knowingly bought them. They turn up at auction houses, in foreign countries, and in private collections. Bibliophiles are known to spend huge sums of money on a single book to complete a collection. They get what they want, legal or not, and at any price. Once purchased, they can squirrel it away forever. You can only imagine the difficulty in tracking down these kinds of anonymous transactions."

"I'm beginning to understand Morrigan's paranoia about his books," he said.

She thumbed through the appraisals, holding them under the light. "Here it is, the Hemingway appraisal. There are two actually: *The Old Man and the Sea,* Scribner, 1952, first edition, signed. The signature is faded, which devalues it some. And here is the 1940 *For Whom the Bell Tolls,* very good condition, slight dust jacket tear, and it's signed. It was appraised at five thousand."

"Now what?"

"To Special Collections," she said. "We have to know for certain that book is in there."

"About this kidnapping thing?" he said.

"I managed to escape," she said, clicking off the light.

***

The door swung open to the Special Collections room, and the flashlight's narrow beam disappeared into the darkness. The air was cool and still, and the windows were covered to admit the smallest light. It felt to Ethan like entering a tomb. Leather-bound tomes rose nearly to the ceiling, frayed and worn by ancient hands and antiquity.

Plush furniture encircled the reading area: leather chairs and reading lamps, a vintage rolltop desk with no apparent function. The east wall housed shelving for early maps, tubes arranged like the comb of giant honey bees. Paintings of bearded men with hard eyes and women with sweeping dresses moved in the shadows. Signs identified the works of Thomas Jefferson and Issac Newton.

"Wait here," Anna said, taking the light.

He waited as she disappeared into the collection. His anxiety rose as he thought about the seriousness of their intrusion into Morrigan's precious books. If they were discovered, there would be no explaining, and he was already in deep with Captain Armen.

Suddenly Anna's light reappeared. "I found the Hemingway material," she said. "Come on back."

He followed her through the shelves, the ferment of old books heavy about them.

"There," she said. "That is correspondence from Hemingway himself, and over there is the copy of *The Old Man and the Sea,* the Scribner edition." She panned the titles one by one with her light. She searched the bottom shelf, then looked up at him. "The 1940 *For Whom the Bell Tolls* is not here."

"Are you sure? Maybe it was not shelved correctly?"

"Morrigan would not shelve any book incorrectly, and certainly not a rare Hemingway. I'm telling you, Ethan, it's gone."

Chapter 25

Anna stepped to her kitchen door. "Something to drink? I have Merlot?"

"After breaking and entering, something more substantial would work."

"Scotch? I might have a bottle somewhere . . ."

"Perfect," he said.

Anna returned with glasses and took up the seat next to him to taste her drink. She wrinkled her nose. "How do you drink this stuff?"

"Practice," he said. He leaned back. "OK, so the Hemingway is gone. The larger question, I guess, is who has access to that collections room?"

"Well, Morrigan, of course, and me."

"OK, so we will eliminate you as a possibility, even though you just told me how much you lusted after that book."

"I don't think *lusted* describes it accurately."

"*Wanted*?"

"We will go with *wanted,* thank you."

"Anyone else?"

Anna set her glass aside as she thought about it. "Well, I don't know. I suppose the board members might on occasion, but Dr. Morrigan is very careful about letting anyone in unsupervised."

"What about the appraisers?"

"Appraisers would have to have access to the books. I mean, they would have knowledge about what books were in the collection, I suppose, but Dr. Morrigan uses professional appraisers."

"Like?"

"Well, like auction houses and antiquarian bookdealers of repute. Credentials can be checked through the American Society of Appraisers."

"What about the public at large? Are they allowed access?"

"Never without supervision."

"Researchers?"

"Not without registration and the personal approval of Dr. Morrigan. They are checked before leaving the collection to make certain no materials are removed."

"And the custodian does not go into Special Collections?"

"Not without supervision, and they don't have a key, as you know."

"And that included Belowe?"

"Yes."

Ethan took another drink of his scotch and set his glass aside. "Maybe he was using the key out of the cabinet, the one we used tonight."

"No one but me knows about that key. It was to be used for emergencies only, like a fire, for example. Dr. Morrigan worries a lot about fire. He would never have issued a key to the Special Collections room to Belowe."

"But Belowe did have a key to the back door and access to the security system. Maybe he was working with someone, someone who had a key to Special Collections?"

"Like who, Ethan? I just told you no one but Morrigan and I have access to a key."

"And you didn't do it?"

"I did not."

"And that leaves?"

"Why would Morrigan steal books from his own collection?"

"I don't know, but he knew the value of that book. He knew where it was, and he had a key." Ethan stood, then sat back down. "How long could it take before anyone discovered such a book was missing?"

"If no one requested it, possibly a good long time, maybe not until the next appraisal process. Maybe not then. Things are updated and sold and traded pretty often.

"And I don't see how Belowe would have anything to do with this either, Ethan. I doubt he knew anything about rare books. How would he have even known which books were the most valuable, which ones to steal?"

"Belowe worked in the Hathaway Building. He had access to that bookstore, as well as to the expertise in it. And he had access to this library. Maybe he discovered something going on and took advantage. Sissy Bluestone said he was good at that. Maybe he was on the take. All I know for sure is that he wound up floating in the lake."

"But to kill him? This is about books, not drugs."

"It's about money, and people die over money all the time."

Anna slid over next to him and rested her arm on his knee. He could feel the tension leave his body. He was wound a little tighter than he'd realized.

"Maybe we should call the police about this," she said.

"Captain Armen? I don't think he would approve, Anna. He's convinced I'm somehow involved."

"We could tell Dr. Morrigan, turn the whole thing over to him?"

"After breaking into the Special Collections room? We'd both be fired by quitting time."

She leaned against his shoulder. Lightning flashed somewhere in the distance, and thunder rumbled across the horizon.

"It's going to rain," he said.

"Ethan?"

"Yes?"

"Maybe there are even more books missing. Maybe there are a lot of them missing. We have no way of knowing for sure."

He reached for his glass on the coffee table. "The answer can't be found with Clarence Belowe—he can no longer speak for himself—but there would have to be more than one person involved in that kind of heist."

"Like?"

"Like there would be the people who have access to the goods, those who sell them, and those who buy them."

"And who would know who does what?" she said. "How do we get inside all that? It's a secret, rarefied world."

Rain began to drum against the window, and lightning lit the room. He watched as it faded into the night, thunder following in a distant rumble.

"If we had someone to go into that bookstore and make a request for a very special book," he said, "maybe we could track the process."

"But who to go?"

"I've always wanted a first-edition, signed Hemingway," he said.

Chapter 26

Ethan had just finished cleaning the first floor of the library and was loading up his cart to move to the second floor when Anna approached. She had an armload of books and motioned him into the stacks.

"We need to talk," she said.

"What's up?"

"I couldn't sleep for thinking about what you said last night, about you posing as a collector at that bookstore."

"We need to get on the inside if we are going to find anything, Anna."

"Look, Dr. Morrigan was gone this morning to a board meeting, so I had a chance to do a little investigating."

Ethan looked over her shoulder to make sure they were still alone. "You've been breaking into the file cabinet again, haven't you?"

"Me, break into the file cabinet? Yes, but don't worry. I was careful."

"I've been thinking about all this myself,

Anna, and there is one thing we've not dealt with here. It's time we talked about it."

"Dr. Morrigan?" she said.

"We don't know how involved he might be. It could be dangerous to ignore the possibility, especially for you. No one has more access to the collection or more knowledge about the market than him. He's the one who knows who is buying and who is selling. No one could alter the appraisals at will like him. All I'm saying is that we have to take a hard look at him too."

Anna frowned. "I've worked with him for years, Ethan. He has personally nourished that collection into what it is. Others have access as well, like the foundation board, which is responsible for oversight, and there is no shortage of expertise among them as well. Don't forget that Dr. Morrigan is an eminently qualified archivist and has spent his life collecting and preserving those rare documents. I can't believe he would be stealing from the collection to make money."

Ethan said, "All I'm saying is that someone killed Clarence Belowe and dumped his body in the lake and that we should be cautious."

"I get it, but we have to be cautious about implicating someone as well. I agree that we need access to that bookstore. I'm confident that Hemingway book is in there. We need to know how it got there, but I also think you underestimate the risk involved."

He shrugged. "I'm a collector looking for a book."

"That's just it, Ethan. Rare book collecting is not that simple. There's a lot to know, and a lot of ways you could be outed."

"You think I'm rare book deficient, don't you?"

"Woefully," she said. "Most collectors spend a lifetime studying their subject. Do you even know what constitutes a rare book?"

"It's an old book that is hard to find."

"That's exactly right, Ethan. There are a lot of old books that are hard to find that are not considered rare; likewise, there are a lot of books that are not old that are considered rare."

"So, you can tell me which books are important for a collection, at least enough for me to be convincing."

"But there are other factors that only informed collectors know. It wouldn't take long for someone to figure out that you are not a collector, at least not one who would be collecting highly valuable books."

"Like what?"

"Like details about first editions, first printings, points, condition, dust jackets, association copies, on and on. You do see what I mean? You could be easily discovered."

He furrowed his brow. "You're saying that I'm not the one to do this?"

"I thought about doing it myself, but I've worked at the library here a long time. There's a good chance that I could be recognized. But if you go to that bookstore pretending to be an expert, you'll be in trouble fast."

"So what do we do?"

"Tell them up front that your knowledge is limited, that you are an agent looking for a specific book for a collector who wishes to remain anonymous. That way, if the questions get sticky, you'll have an out."

"Good plan," he said. "So, what book am I looking for?"

"When we went through the Hemingway collection, there was a signed 1952 first edition of *The Old Man and the Sea,* Scribner. Do you remember?"

"Sort of."

She cocked her head. "Ethan, this is serious."

"*The Old Man and the Sea,* Scribner."

"I looked up the appraised value this morning. That copy is priced at around two thousand, mostly because of the condition. You could keep your search to that one book so as not to raise suspicion. The first printing has the letter 'A' on the copyright page. OK? Insist on the olive jacket, because that's what's in our collection. Got it?"

"Got it," he said. "I'll go to the store after work today. I'll come by your place tonight, if that's OK?"

She walked to the door, then turned. "Ethan, be careful. We have no idea how deep this could run."

He stood at the front door of the bookstore for some time, screwing up his courage. Going in was harder than he'd anticipated. Anna was right. It was a world he knew precious little about.

"To hell with it," he said to himself. He took a deep breath and stepped in.

The girl at the desk looked up from her book. She wore gold, dangling earrings and a

1930s haircut. She smiled, a practiced smile, the kind reserved for customers.

"May I help you?" she said.

"My name is Ross Bosley. I'm searching for a particular rare book. Is there someone I could talk to?"

"Mr. Cherney is in the back. I can call him. What did you say your name is?"

"Ross Bosley."

She laid her book aside and picked up the phone. Ethan looked around. The store was nearly empty. Rare book collectors were probably as rare as the books they coveted. That would make finding a customer rare as well.

"Mr. Bosley," the girl said, "Mr. Cherney can see you now. The rare book section is at the back of the store. He will let you in."

"Thank you."

A pear-shaped man in his fifties was waiting at the side door of the collections room. He was bald and pale and older than Ethan remembered, so pale in fact that there was the possibility that he'd never been exposed to actual sunlight. Tortoiseshell glasses hung around his neck, leaving little doubt that it was the same guy Anna and he had seen that day they were there browsing. Ethan waited as Cherney unlocked the door.

Cherney, smelling heavily of cologne, stuck out his hand. "Mr. Bosley," he said.

For a second, Ethan failed to recognize his own alias. "Yes, yes," he said. "Ross Bosley. Nice meeting you."

"Baden Cherney. Come in, won't you?" Cherney said, stepping aside. "Could I get you something to drink, coffee perhaps?"

"Yes, I believe I will. Black, please."

"Have a seat, Mr. Bosley," he said. "I'll be right with you."

Ethan glanced around the room while he waited. There were no windows, and many of the books were protected with archival covers. He could feel the coolness of the controlled humidity, and there was the slightly fermented smell of ancient paper. The atmosphere reminded him of old cathedrals he'd visited once while on a European vacation.

Cherney returned with coffee mugs and took up a seat across from him. "Have you been in our store before?" he asked.

"First time," Ethan said. "Though your reputation is stellar."

"Thank you. We do our best. Operating a

rare book store requires considerable time and attention. You see, reputation is everything in this business."

"Collectors are a bit eccentric, I suppose," Ethan said, smiling.

"Indeed," he said, "but it's that very fastidiousness that makes this business special, as you must know."

Ethan took a sip of his coffee, black and rich. "I have a confession to make," he said.

"Oh?"

"I'm not a collector, you see."

"Then what is it you want here, Mr. Bosley?"

"I'm representing someone else, actually. I have been hired to research possible purchases for a client. Whether he buys or declines a product is strictly up to him, of course."

"You are not a collector yourself then?"

"That is correct. My client wishes to remain anonymous."

"I see. Is this for an institution or a private collection?"

"Is that necessary to know?"

"Only for tax purposes, that is, exempt purchases. That would be up to you in any event. Please tell your client that his anonymity is assured here. We deal with that request quite often in this business. Sometimes it's helpful to know where an item is going in order to fully assure privacy about the transaction."

"I'd rather not divulge that kind of information at this time."

"I understand. Collectors can be quite guarded. They are all a bit secretive. I do use the term in the nicest possible way."

"Secretive? How do you mean?"

Cherney pushed his cup aside and folded his hands in his lap. "Well, they are all very much similar in their passion for whatever it is that they are collecting. Their exact motivation is not always apparent, though they tend to be highly competitive."

"What do you mean?"

"Why that particular book? Why you? I've asked the question of them many times. The answers vary to some degree, but for many it is connected to their past, a recollection of a special moment or person, for example. For others it appears to be genetic or formed through tradition. It's hard to distinguish which at times. And then, of course, a few are driven by the investment. I must say *that* motivation is best understood by the rest of us normal people.

"You see, the intensity of a collector's passion can be quite extraordinary, whether it's collecting rare books or miniature turtles or some other obscurity. Whatever it is that they desire, they must have it, and at any cost."

"Are you suggesting that they have to be wealthy to collect?"

"Or find alternatives. Unfortunately, it is sometimes at the cost of a marriage, or the dissolution of a family, or the bottom line of a business. But never assume that they do not fully understand what it is they are searching for. They know exactly what it is they want, and they will settle for nothing less.

"With rare books, condition is everything for a collector—well, not everything, but it often sets the bottom line. There is provenance, of course, and literary reputation, and autographs and associations. Whatever the criteria are, they must be met, and that is where we come in. We know how to meet demands, and that includes the need for anonymity."

"I didn't fully realize that some people could be so driven to read a book."

Cherney smiled. "Oh, it isn't about reading, Mr. Bosley. It's about having. And now that you understand the rules of the game, what exactly is your client looking for?"

"He has an extensive war writers collection that he wants to complete. He's interested in Hemingway."

"We have several nice Hemingways available."

"He's especially interested in procuring a copy of *The Old Man and the Sea*."

"Well, we have several available, but knowing collectors, I'm sure he was more specific."

"First edition, first printing, the one with the 'A' on the copyright page."

"Yes, I thought there might be more."

"He also asked that it have the olive-colored dust jacket. He emphasized that it must be the olive jacket."

Cherney slipped his glasses on, and his eyes grew large. The strings hanging from his glasses gave him a distinctly scholarly appearance. "That does narrow the field. Let me see what we have."

Cherney went to his files and thumbed through the folders. When he returned, he said, "I'm afraid we don't have that particular book in stock at the moment. Is there something else we could interest you in?"

"Just *The Old Man and the Sea,* as far as

I know," he said. "My man was quite adamant that it meet those requirements."

"I see. We do have a nice copy of *For Whom the Bell Tolls.* It's a signed first edition. We could make an exclusive offer. You did say war writers. No book fits that description better. Perhaps your client would be interested? Is he concerned about who is selling? It could make a difference on availability and price."

Ethan stood. "I could check, Mr. Cherney. He's completing a much larger personal collection and would not be selling in the future. If he's satisfied with its authenticity, I don't think he would be particularly concerned about its history."

"You could leave your phone number with the girl up front. I'll do some checking and give you a call if we locate the specified copy."

"Thank you. For your information, my client does have the means to acquire what he wants, and he prefers paying in cash."

Mr. Cherney let his glasses drop back down. "I see. Please tell him that we do have the means to clean a book if necessary, Mr. Bosley."

"Ah, yes," Ethan said, going to the door. "I'll pass the information along. Thank you for your time."

***

Despite the waning hour, Ethan drove to Anna's house and knocked on the front door. She opened it wearing pajamas with red-and-white laughing clowns on them. Her hair was tumbling over her shoulders.

"You said it would be OK if I came," he said.

"I'm glad you did. I don't think I could sleep wondering how it went." She switched on a small lamp next to the couch. "Tell me."

"The owner's name is Baden Cherney. I told him what we were looking for, emphasizing the points that we talked about. He didn't have the book on hand but said he would be on the lookout. I told him that money was not an issue for my client. He was particularly interested in knowing that my client was a private collector and that the book would not be placed back on the market. My name is Ross Bosley, by the way."

"Very original, Ross."

"He wanted to know if my client was concerned about who might be selling. I told him not so much. Then he said something I didn't quite understand."

"What?"

"He said that his business had the professional skills to clean a book. Why would you clean a book? I thought they were to be kept as original as possible."

Anna looked at him. "It means they can remove identifying markings."

"Markings?"

"Any kind of unwanted markings, including library stamps, magnetic strips, anything that might associate the book with a given institution or collection. Once it's cleaned, there's no way to trace its origin."

"He said he would call if he came up with something." Ethan stood and walked to the door. "It's late, Anna, and tomorrow is a workday. I just wanted to let you know. I better be on my way."

"I can't help but wonder if there are other books missing," she said. "The whole collection could be at risk, and if the inventory is inaccurate—"

"So, where do we go from here?"

"If *The Old Man and the Sea* turns up missing from Special Collections, we will know something is going on. Until then, we wait."

Chapter 27

And wait they did, for two weeks. During that wait, Ethan mopped bathrooms, swept floors, and cleaned offices. He tried to do the office cleaning in early mornings or late in the day to avoid interfering with business.

Often he would leave the building at noon and take his lunch to the car to eat, just to escape for a bit. On occasion he would go on a brisk walk, usually past the school where he'd taught that one, brief semester. The truth was that he'd grown increasingly discontented with the custodial work. Although it was honest work, it lacked intellectual challenge and interaction with people, something he missed more than he'd anticipated.

On one occasion he ran across a colleague from the school, a social studies teacher with whom he'd shared lunch hours. He'd filled him in on all the latest gossip, who had done what to whom. When his friend asked what he was doing now, Ethan told him that he was going back to school to work on his master's degree. Though it wasn't true, it was something he'd entertained and so was not *exactly* a lie.

The truth was that his relationship with Anna had grown increasingly close. He found himself drawn to her more all the time, taken with her intelligence, her sense of humor, and her determination. But each time he'd considered acting on his feelings, images of Olivia, filled with anger and deception, came rushing back to him. It had been impossible to overcome the memory, and none of it was fair to Anna.

***

The call they'd been waiting for came on one of those lunch break walks. He was a block from the library when his cell phone rang. He stepped into the shade of an old elm to escape the noon heat.

"Hello?" he said.

"Mr. Bosley?" a girl said.

He hesitated, then answered. "Yes, this is he."

"I'm calling with regard to a book you requested at our shop a couple weeks ago."

His pulse ticked up. "Oh, yes," he said.

"Mr. Cherney has located a copy that meets your specifications. He asked that I contact you. Would you care to come in and examine the book?"

"Well, yes. I could come in later today. Would that work?"

"Just a moment, and I'll check." He could hear her talking to someone, their voices muffled. When she came back on, she said, "Would six today be OK with you? The store is open until nine."

"Six? Yes. I'll be there. Thank you for calling."

***

He caught Anna at the water fountain and motioned for her to come to the basement. Minutes later, she came in and leaned against the wall.

"What's up? " she asked.

"I got the call," he said. "I'm to go in at six o'clock today."

"He has the book?"

"He has *a* book. Whether it's from Special Collections remains to be seen."

"Oh, God, Ethan, if it *is,* something will have to be done."

"But what?" he said.

"I don't know, not just yet. We'll make that decision if we have to. This could still be a legit transaction. The whole thing scares the hell out of me, though. "

He looked at her. "I have a small problem."

"What problem?"

"I don't have the money to buy it."

"Oh, for heaven's sake, what kind of con man are you?"

"A shortsighted one. So, what do we do?"

She stood silently for a moment. "Look the book over. Tell him you will need to talk to your client and that you will get back with him. In the meantime, we can check our inventory. We may not need money at this point."

"Another breaking and entering job, I assume?"

"No breaking, just entering. I can get the key, remember? If that copy is missing, we'll know for certain that the collection is being plundered."

***

Mr. Cherney dropped his head to the side and peered through the window before letting Ethan in to the rare book room.

"Glad you could make it, Mr. Bosley. It's a nice copy. Any collector would be proud to have it in his possession. Please have a seat, and I will bring it out."

Ethan took his place at the table and waited for Cherney to return. He could see the girl at the front, her lips pursed as she refreshed her lipstick in a compact mirror.

Cherney returned with the Hemingway, laid it out in front of him, and opened the book to the copyright page. He smelled slightly of stale coffee. He sat down across from Ethan and folded his hands in front of him.

"It's a 1952 Scribner," he said, "first printing, with signature, just like you requested." He closed the book and tapped it with his finger. "Olive jacket too. I was quite surprised we could come up with that one. They're very rare, you know."

"Is it a married jacket?" Ethan asked with authority, having learned the term from Anna. In fact, he'd picked up quite a bit of the jargon over the weeks.

"Original. You can see the fit has wear."

"Clean?"

"This copy could go into a private collection without questions," he said.

Ethan examined the copy. Closing it, he said, "What is the price?"

"Two thousand, cash, a bargain."

"That's a little high," Ethan said. "And the signature has deteriorated. It appears to have been signed with a ballpoint. They fade over time, you know. My client is particular about such things. I need to check with him, make certain that it's acceptable."

Cherney's ears reddened. "When will you know? I have another client waiting, you see."

"I'll get back to you soon," he said. "If you have someone in the wings, please feel free to sell the copy. I wouldn't expect you to hold it."

Cherney slid back in his chair. "Does your client collect only war writers, Mr. Bosley?"

Ethan hesitated, uncertain as to the point of the question. "He collects several things," he said. "What did you have in mind?"

"Presidential books, perhaps?"

"It depends."

"I also have access to a very nice *The Maltese Falcon* by Hammett."

"Signed?"

"Yes. He is quite collectible, you know, and his signature is highly desirable."

"It isn't available for me to see now?" he asked.

"I don't have it in hand, but we do have contacts. Arrangements could be made. Do you think your client would be interested?"

"Possibly. I will let him know."

He picked up the Hemingway. "The dust jacket is original, as you can see, Mr. Bosley. Such material is quite valuable, and the demand is high. But we would entertain a fair offer by your client."

Ethan stood. "Thank you. I'll be in touch, Mr. Cherney."

As he made his way to the exit, he could see someone talking to the clerk at the front, a girl leaning in on her elbows. When he went by, she looked over her shoulder.

"Oh, hi, Mr. Poser," she said. "How are you?"

He nodded. "Fine, thank you."

When he was on the street and headed back to Anna's house, he realized what had just transpired. The girl who had spoken to him was Mia Layla, from Anna's book club.

***

Anna sat down next to him on the couch. "Are you sure it was Mia?"

"There is no doubt. She spoke to me as I was leaving the bookstore. It took me a moment to realize who she was."

"She must see people she knows all the time in the mall," Anna said. "I don't think there's a need for concern."

"She called me Mr. Poser in front of the bookstore clerk."

"Clerks don't pay any attention to people's names, Ethan. I don't think there's a need to worry. So, tell me what happened with Cherney."

"It was the correct Hemingway. I'm certain of it, right down to the color of the jacket. I told him I'd have to talk with my client about the condition and the price."

"What was he asking for it?"

"Two thousand. I suggested it was a bit high. He is willing to bargain."

She bobbed her foot. "He's proud of it, isn't he?"

"And that isn't all," he said.

She dropped her chin and looked at him.

"There's more?"

"Cherney asked if my client would be interested in *The Maltese Falcon.* He didn't have it on hand but said he has a contact, that it wouldn't come cheap, that it was highly collectible."

Anna was quiet for several moments. Looking over at him, she said, "We have *The Maltese Falcon* in Special Collections, Ethan."

"Yes," he said, "I thought we might."

Chapter 28

Ethan and Anna parked in the shadows at the back of the library's parking lot in the hope that no one would spot the car. There was little he could do about the security light that lit up the back door, except pray that no one was watching. He searched his pockets for the door key.

"Damn it," he said.

"What's the matter?" Anna said, whispering.

"I left the library key at home."

Anna looked back at the car. "How could you do that?"

"Did you bring yours?"

She searched her purse. "Yes, here it is, thank goodness. Now hurry, please."

He unlocked the door, and they stepped in. Anna waited for him to disarm the alarm system. The silence of the old building closed in about them. Ethan could hear Anna breathing in the darkness behind him. He clicked on his flashlight, and she joined him at his side. They made their way to the office, where Anna retrieved the key to Special Collections. As they climbed the stairs to the mezzanine, a siren rose up from somewhere downtown. Anna took his arm.

"Ethan . . ."

"Probably a fire truck," he said.

Anna unlocked the door to the Special Collections room, and they paused for a moment. Entering the forbidden space was eerie. There was something mystical in the presence of all those rare books.

"Now where?" he said, panning the room with his light.

"First we check to see if *The Old Man and the Sea* is still here," she said. "It should be over there. If not, it's likely to be on sale now at Cherney's shop."

He followed her into the stacks, where she knelt and scanned the shelves with the flashlight. She looked up at him, then scanned them again.

Standing, she said, "It's gone, Ethan."

"Are you sure?"

She scanned again, slower this time, reading the titles out as she went. "*The Old Man and the Sea* is not here. Both of our most valuable Hemingway copies are missing."

"What about the Hammett?"

"It would be in the cabinet at the very back." She took his hand, and he could feel her trembling. "What if it's gone too?" she said. "*The Maltese Falcon* is one of our most valued books."

"At least we will know where to look for it."

They edged their way back to the cabinet, where he held the light as she searched for the Hammett. She turned, and he could see the tears in her eyes.

"Well?"

"It should be right here, Ethan. I remember seeing it."

"Look again," he said. "We need to be certain."

Sweat trickled down his neck as he waited. Finally, he asked, "Nothing?"

She stood, turning to him. "Gone."

"The Hammett's gone? You're sure?"

"*The Maltese Falcon* is gone," she said. He could hear the tension in her voice. "Do you know what this means, Ethan?" She didn't wait for an answer. "That book was last appraised at twenty-five thousand dollars. How could this have happened?"

"Twenty-five thousand? I can understand

how someone might wind up dead under a pier now. Come on, let's get out of here."

They groped their way out of Special Collections and down the stairs to the back door. Ethan was setting the security alarm when Anna said, "Wait, I forgot something."

"What?"

"I didn't return the key to the collections room."

"Can't you put it back tomorrow?"

"No, Ethan, what if it were discovered missing? Anyway, I'm not sure I locked the cabinet either."

They found it unlocked, just as she'd thought. She put the key back, and minutes later they were at the exit door once again. Anna held the light while Ethan reset the security alarm, its shrill beep fracturing their nerves as it began its countdown.

They exited into the fresh night air, anxious to leave behind the crushing truth of the missing volumes. But just as they turned for the car, a man stepped out from the shadows, his shoulders squared.

"Fancy meeting you two here," Captain Armen said, holding his badge out under the parking lot light.

***

Ethan and Anna rode in the back seat of Captain Armen's car. Armen's neck looked like the tooled pattern of an old leather saddle.

"We can explain," Ethan said.

Captain Armen held up his hand for Ethan to stop. "I'd as soon you wait until we get to the station, Mr. Poser, because I have a feeling that what you're about to say is going to require my full attention."

***

Ethan and Anna sat in Captain Armen's office and waited as he opened his notebook. He flipped through the pages and looked up.

"Now," he said, "suppose you tell me what you were doing coming out of the library at two o'clock in the morning?"

Ethan glanced at Anna. "You're not going to believe this," he said.

"Try me, Mr. Poser. You'd be surprised at the stories I've heard over the course of my career."

"Anna and I were at Hathaway's Used and

Rare Books a while back, just browsing, you might say."

"Or nosing around about Clarence Belowe," he said. "Go on with your story, Mr. Poser."

"We were at the back of the store where they have their rare books when Anna happened to notice a Hemingway book, *For Whom the Bell Tolls,* she thought she recognized as having been in Special Collections at the library."

Captain Armen turned to Anna. "How exactly did you *recognize* it, Ms. Khole?"

"It had a small dust jacket tear," she said. "I thought it looked like the same tear as our copy in Special Collections."

"You recognized a small tear? Quite observant, isn't it, Ms. Khole?"

"A dust jacket tear is a significant issue in the rare book business, Captain. It can make a substantial difference in the value of a book."

Captain Armen wrote something in his notebook. "And so you looked in the library's Special Collections to see if it was missing?"

"Yes."

"And was it?"

She nodded. "Hemingway had signed it as well. Anyway, in an effort to make certain we weren't making a mistake, we decided to request a different Hemingway title from Hathaway's, *The Old Man and the Sea*."

"Which was also in Special Collections?"

"Yes," Ethan said. "I claimed to be an agent for a client. The bookstore just happened to know where a book like that might be purchased."

Captain Armen stood and walked to the window. He turned. "So tonight you were checking to see if that book was missing as well?"

"Yes," Ethan said. "And it is. Someone is systematically stealing the books and fencing them through Hathaway's bookstore."

"That's not all," Anna said. "*The Maltese Falcon* by Hammett is missing too."

"How much?"

"Twenty-five."

"Thousand? What is to keep people from just walking out with all the library books at will?"

Anna said, "All library books are barcoded, and if they aren't demagnetized when they're checked out, an alarm goes off as they pass through the front door. Special Collections books are not barcoded. It tends to damage the books."

"And the back door?"

"There's only the security alarm," Ethan said. "But nothing specifically for books."

"So someone *could* take books out the back?"

Ethan answered, "They would need a key to get into the Special Collections room and the know-how to get out the back door."

"And they would need to know how to disarm the security system, the right code," Anna said.

"And who has keys to Special Collections?" he asked.

"I do, and Dr. Morrigan," Anna said.

"And the back door alarm code?"

"Dr. Morrigan, Ethan, and I know the code."

"So, the only people who can access Special Collections are you and Dr. Morrigan? You each have a key?"

"Only Dr. Morrigan has a key," she said. "But there is an extra key in his file cabinet in the office that I can access."

"So you can get into Special Collections by using the spare key?"

"Yes," Anna said.

"And Clarence Belowe would have had the same security arrangement as Mr. Poser?"

"Yes," Anna said.

"Would Belowe have had access to the office where the spare key resides?"

"Yes," she said. "The custodians are responsible for cleaning the offices, but the key is well hidden."

Captain Armen clicked his pen in and out as he thought. "Exactly what is the total value of Special Collections, Ms. Khole?"

"Somewhere around twelve million."

He lowered his chin. "And you have no idea how many of these books are missing?"

Anna glanced at Ethan. "We don't know for certain."

"What's the higher-end dollar on these books?" Armen asked.

"The collection has a book once owned by Thomas Jefferson."

"And its value?"

"Two hundred and twenty-five thousand."

Armen said, "Good Lord."

"And of course there's Newton's *Principia,*" she said. "It approaches a million dollars."

"A million dollars?"

Ethan said, "Here's the thing, Captain. We've been bluffing our way through this because we don't have the funds to buy from Hathaway's. Without dealing, we are never going to be able to track who's involved, and Cherney is going to get suspicious at some point."

Armen pitched his pen onto the desk. "Come on, I'll take you to your car."

They drove in silence on the way back to the library. When Armen had pulled up next to Ethan's car, he looked in the rearview mirror and said, "Go back to work as usual and don't say a word to anyone about all this. I will be in touch."

"Captain," Ethan said.

"What?"

"How did you know we were in the library?"

"I didn't," he said. "I was called out about some Mexican fellow sleeping on the library steps."

Chapter 29

Anna sat upright in bed. She stared into the darkness. At times her dreams were too stark to bear. The missing rare books, and her own implication in the situation, were a nightmare.

She wondered at her ineptitude in not knowing what was happening, her inattention, especially given her personal awareness of the money involved. Clarence Belowe had been in her office many times, most often when she wasn't present. She could only imagine Dr. Morrigan's reaction when he found out about the missing books.

As for Captain Armen, she would just have to wait and see whether she was in serious trouble with him. He held everything close and was difficult to read. Although Ethan was implicated, he bore much less personal responsibility for the failure than she did, as the associate librarian.

Unable to get back to sleep, she reached for the book that Doris Gill, the aging widow, had selected for the book club. It was titled *Every Last One* by Anna Quindlen. Even though the book was dated, she'd said nothing about that to Doris. She had given them free rein to select a title that mattered in their lives, and she intended to stay true to that commitment, even though not everyone in the club would relate to the same book in the same way. To date, most of the members had been tolerant of their differences.

***

When Anna arrived at work the next morning, the library was open, and all the lights were on, which meant that Ethan had arrived early himself. The first thing she did was check the file cabinet and make sure everything was still secured. After that, she worked on shelving book returns, where she spotted Diego Pinto in one of the carrels. He was wearing headphones and was deeply engaged with the material. She hoped he could keep his reading deficit from the others, but it would be a challenging task to accomplish in a room full of widely read book club members. He was trying hard to fit in, and she didn't want him discouraged.

After lunch, Dr. Morrigan stopped by her office and asked about the progress of the book club.

"The membership is growing nicely," she said. "And we have chosen a name for it."

"I hope it isn't one of those cute things," he said. "A book club should have a scholarly name."

"We've decided on Book Club Central, you know, because of our position in the system."

He paused, dropping his chin as he thought it over. Anna had never before noticed the birthmark hidden in the gray hair above his ear. He grunted his approval and pointed to the front door. "Someone has been sleeping on the steps of the library again. See to it, will you?"

***

That evening, Diego Pinto was the first to arrive at the Genealogy Room for the club meeting. Anna thought he looked tired, and he was unshaven.

"Hello, Diego," she said. "How are you?"
"I am good," he said. "Very good."
"Are you sure, Diego?"
"Yes, yes," he said. "I am too good."

"Have you found employment yet?"

"Employment?"

"Have you found work yet?"

"I'm waiting to hear about the next big job," he said.

"What kind of work did you have in Mexico?"

"I was a security officer in a bank," he said. "For many years I did this work."

"Have you tried to find such work here in America?"

"*Sí,* in many places, but they say immigrants cannot be trusted with such important things. They say we will steal from them back."

"I have been wondering, Diego. You haven't seen anyone sleeping on the steps of the library, have you? I know you would have noticed."

"Oh, no," he said. "It is not a place for sleeping."

"The thing is, while it doesn't matter personally to me, the authorities have been alerted. I wouldn't want anyone to get into trouble."

"That would be a very bad thing. I will watch to make sure no one sleeps on the steps. They must find some other place."

After they'd gathered for the meeting, Anna checked the roll. Everyone showed up except Dakota Chance and Mia Layla. She waited another five minutes, then started without them.

She said, "Tonight Doris Gill will be presenting her take on *Every Last One* by Anna Quindlen. Doris, would you come to the podium, please?"

Doris lifted out of her chair and made her way to the front. Slightly overweight, and with a decided limp, she moved slowly and deliberately.

"Good evening," she said, adjusting her glasses. "I chose this book because, as some of you know, I lost my husband, and this book is all about grief, you know, grieving the loss of someone you dearly loved.

"What I liked about the book is that it also tells about the loneliness and isolation that follow the death of someone, how the world sees the loss, and how they treat you differently because of it. People hide what they are thinking because they are afraid of what you will feel. They don't talk about the person you lost or say his name or remember the things he said and did when he was alive. They are afraid that the memories will cause pain, but the memories are what you have left, the only thing you have left, don't you see?"

She looked around the room. "Not only

has that person suffered a great loss, a sorrow that never goes away, but now they must also hide their own feelings. This is what this book is about. Anyone who has lost someone should read it. Anyone who *loses* someone should read it and consider the emptiness, blackness, and hopelessness that can follow.

"But they should also know that nothing has changed with death except the absence of that person. For example, all the things that I loved about my husband, I still love, even though he is gone. I don't want to forget or hide those things. I don't want you to forget them either. I want to remember. I want to hear his name spoken.

"For me, that's what this book is about," she said. "It's about death, loneliness, and the sweetness of memories."

"What was your husband's name?" Anna asked.

"His name was Bert. Everyone called him Bertie."

"Remember Bertie," Anna said.

Doris's eyes filled, and she put her hand on her heart.

Imani Bell held up her hand. "I lost my mother this year," she said. "I hear her voice sometimes, and I remember the smell of her kitchen."

"What was her name?" Anna asked.

"Missy," she said. "That's what we called her."

And so one by one they shared the memories and spoke the names of lost loved ones, to bring them back, if only for a moment. Even Van Number, the old bachelor who clerked at the bank, held up his hand. He spoke of a beautiful young girl and of unrequited love. He lowered his eyes and clasped his hands as they joined to remember her.

And then Anna spoke herself, asking the group to remember Danny, her little brother, who had died so tragically only a few blocks from where they now gathered.

When everyone had finished, Anna looked around the room. They were no longer strangers but friends. Tears flowed down many faces. If nothing else, the book club members had taken a moment to share the loneliness that each had experienced in one way or another.

The room was filled with memories. The only one who hadn't spoken was Diego Pinto, who sat on the back row.

"Anyone else care to participate?" she asked.

Diego lowered his head and clasped his hands together in his lap.

Anna said, "OK, then that concludes our meeting. I'm proud of your participation. Read your next selection, and I'll see everyone next time."

***

Ethan was waiting to walk home with Anna when she came out. "How did it go tonight?" he asked.

"Great," she said. "Doris did a wonderful job."

She wanted to tell him what they had done, but it was something that was difficult to share, not without diminishing the moment somehow.

They exited the back door and were headed homeward when Anna spotted Diego and Doris standing under the streetlight across the lot. Diego drew Doris in and gave her a hug. They waved goodbye to each other and went their separate ways.

"Diego?" Ethan said.

She nodded. "He and Doris have become good friends. The group has really bonded. By the way, Diego has been sleeping on the library steps, you know. I worry about his safety, and I've talked to him about it. The problem is the poor guy doesn't have any place else to go."

"Would you care to stop at my camper for a drink or something before you go home?"

"I'd like that," she said. "I don't want to be alone just yet."

***

They sat on the couch having their drinks and watching the evening news on Ethan's midget-sized television. Though the camper was small, it had the coziness and warmth of home. Ethan had leaned back and closed his eyes when a knock came at the door. Startled, he sat up. Anna reached for her shoes and slipped them on.

"Who could that be this late?" she asked.

Ethan went to the door to find Captain Armen leaning against the railing in his uniform—an immaculate blue, and with stitched creases. A gold-and-silver badge pinned to his chest announced his authority, which was hardly necessary, given that Armen was larger than life anyway, what with his huge arms and a scar that pulled at the corner of his mouth. His eyes were cold black and unflinching as well.

"Captain," Ethan said. "Is something wrong?"

"Hope I'm not disturbing anything," he said, smiling. "May I come in?"

Ethan stepped back from the doorway. "Please do, Captain. We're just having a little nightcap."

Captain Armen bent under the door, and the room shrank in his presence. "Ms. Khole," he said, taking off his hat.

"Oh, it's you, Captain," Anna said, adjusting her hair.

"Sit down," Ethan said. "May I fix you something to drink?"

Armen squeezed in at the kitchen table, arranging his legs to the side to fit. "No, thanks. I'm good." Ethan sat back down next to Anna. "What is it, Captain? What's going on?"

"Having had a chance to think about this book business, I have a few questions I need cleared up."

"Ask away," Ethan said.

"Now, as I understand it, you are confident that two of your Hemingway books are missing from Special Collections and are in the hands of Hathaway's. Would that be correct?"

"Yes, Hathaway's," Anna said. "It's not far from the library, actually."

"I came across it while tracking down Clarence Belowe's history," Armen said. "He was employed there at one time." He paused. "And you say that the owner offered to sell to you, correct?"

"Yes," Ethan said. "As I mentioned earlier, I told Cherney at the bookstore that my client was interested in owning Hemingway's *The Old Man and the Sea.* Shortly after that, it disappeared from Special Collections. What exactly are you getting at, Captain?"

Armen turned in his seat, and the camper rocked. "Give me the details on the book negotiations."

"He's asking two thousand dollars," Ethan said. "I'm to talk to my client to see if he's interested in a deal. Cherney threw out a tease on a Hammett as well. It's ten times the price of the Hemingway. Needless to say, we won't be dealing on any of them, even the Hemingway. The problem is money. We don't have any, and I'm not sure how long I can stall him."

Armen adjusted his gun belt and hooked his elbows on the table. "I'm not one to trust folks up front," he said. "I've been in this business too long for that. But we got a chance to nail something big here. All we have to do is turn this nibble into a bite."

"What are you getting at?" Ethan asked.

"I've arranged for some cash for an offer on that Hemingway book, *The Old Man and the Ocean.*"

"*Sea,*" Ethan said.

"Excuse me?"

"*The Old Man and the Sea.*"

"Right. And the asking price is two thousand, correct?"

Ethan looked at Anna. "That's what he's asking. A little negotiation is expected, however. It would be unusual for a client to jump at an asking price. I could work him for a while."

"I'm sticking my neck out here pretty damn far," Armen said. "But I'm prepared to provide the money. It's all to be repaid, of course, when we've put this guy in wrappers."

"Not to be too nosy, Captain, but where is this money coming from?"

"The department has a drug account, you know, for setting up drug deals. I've got permission to use it to keep this book thing active. Just so you know, I don't like to get ripped off. I don't like it at all."

"So, where do we go from here, then?" Ethan asked.

"Ms. Khole, would you run off a copy of that collection appraisal for me?" he said. "Ethan, I'll be waiting with the cash after work on Friday. In the meantime, call up this Hathaway's bookstore guy. Tell him you want to deal on that Hemingway. While you're at it, show a little interest in the Hammett as well. That ought keep 'em interested in us."

Chapter 30

Friday morning, Ethan arrived at work early to have a moment to himself before starting. It was his way of getting organized, of thinking things through. The library was quiet that early, and it gave him the opportunity to have a cup of coffee alone in his shop as well. He was to make an appointment with the book dealer Cherney and then meet with Captain Armen after work to pick up the money.

He thought about Captain Armen's concern about the unusual amounts of cash Belowe had deposited into his account. He was beginning to understand that Armen was pretty damn sharp when it came down to it. He'd tracked down Belowe's past fast and well.

But there was still a lot they didn't know. More books could be missing from the collection. Apparently the world was awash in collectors willing to break the law to get what they wanted, and a lot of what they wanted was up there on that mezzanine.

He was beginning to understand that discretion was necessary across a large number of people who might be involved. Not only did the books have to be taken from the collection undetected but they had to be sold to a select clientele. These were not common thieves but highly sophisticated and informed people who had mastered a complicated field. In the end, reputation and trust were essential.

That would surely have excluded Belowe as an actor, him being an untrustworthy soul. On the other hand, being in the right place with the right keys might have been even more important than discretion. The fact that he was dead suggested that such an assumption could have been fatal.

Ethan checked the time, gathered up his things, and headed for the stairs just as Diego appeared.

"Ethan," Diego said, "have you been sleeping in the basement? It's against the law to sleep in the library."

"I've been having my coffee and thinking things over."

"I have many things to think on too," Diego said.

"You are a complicated person, Diego."

"Because I read so many big books, Ethan. I have many words in my head to bump into each other."

"Maybe you should write them in a book of your own to empty your head, Diego, but then, having an empty head has its own drawbacks."

"You should try reading books too, Ethan, then you would know so much as me. It's better than sweeping floors."

"How did I ever get along without your wisdom, I wonder?"

Diego twisted his mouth to the side. "It's a question I have asked many times. But you are a friend and much in need of wisdom, so I give it to you free."

"And I thank you for your generosity, but I do need to get to work now." He paused. "Why are you down here, Diego? Have you started smoking again?"

"I am still quit smoking, but I like bananas very much."

"I see. My lunch sack is over there, but leave my sandwich alone, if you please."

Ethan left Diego to his banana and headed upstairs to begin his day. He worked his way through the first and second floors, his mind disengaged by routine. At noon, he contacted

Hathaway's bookstore and arranged a meeting with Cherney for six thirty that evening.

It was four o'clock by the time he made it to the mezzanine. At that time of day it was almost always absent of people. A bench located under the south window was on occasion occupied by a dozing transient, or by himself. Custodial work could be tiring. Often by this time of day, he was more than ready to sit for a rest. The fact that there was only a single bench was not by accident but Dr. Morrigan's way of discouraging patrons from loitering near his beloved collection.

Ethan sat down, propped his dust mop against the bench, and leaned his head back. He closed his eyes for a brief moment. He was tired but stressed at what lay ahead. In that moment he thought he heard voices coming from the restroom, men's voices, hushed and furtive. He stood, turning his head, and he heard them again, louder this time.

Not wanting to be seen, he picked up his dust mop and stepped back from sight. From his vantage he could just make out two men standing at the restroom entrance. One reached into his pocket and handed something to the other, who in turn headed for the stairs.

When he'd disappeared down the stairs, the other man moved under the exit light. And in that moment Ethan recognized him as Dakota Chance, Mia's boyfriend from the book club.

Ethan checked his watch and waited until they had cleared the building. He'd dozed longer than he'd realized and was running late for his appointment with the book dealer. He paused at the head of the stairwell and looked back at the restroom. Odd, he thought, but not his problem. Turning out the lights, he headed downstairs to close up and be on his way.

***

He'd set the security alarm at the back door and was walking toward his car when he spotted Captain Armen parked at the back of the library lot. He was wearing aviator sunglasses. Ethan walked over to the captain's car and waited for him to roll down the window.

"You get the appointment?" Armen asked.

"I'm on my way there now."

Armen handed him the cash in an envelope and said, "Don't wind up empty-handed, Poser. My job is at stake here."

Ethan started to leave, then hesitated.

"Captain," he said, "there's this fellow by the name of Dakota Chance from Anna's book club."

"Yeah? What about him?"

"I just spotted him and another guy on the mezzanine. It was late, you know."

"Where Special Collections is?"

"Yes. They were coming out of the bathroom."

"What's your point, Poser?"

"Nothing, I suppose, except they exchanged something. I couldn't tell what."

"Maybe a book?" Armen said. "It is a library, ain't it?"

"Yeah, I'm a little uptight about all this, I guess."

Armen looked up at him, the sun reflecting in his sunglasses. "What was that name again?"

"Dakota Chance," he said. "Wears an earring. Hangs with a girl by the name of Mia. They're in Anna's book club."

"We'll talk later," Armen said, rolling up his window.

***

The clerk at Hathaway's was applying lipstick when Ethan came in. She pressed her lips together and dropped the lipstick tube into her purse.

"May I help you?" she asked.

"I have an appointment with Mr. Cherney," Ethan said.

"What was the name again?" she asked.

"Ross Bosley. I called earlier."

"Oh, yes, Mr. Bosley. Mr. Cherney is expecting you. Go on back."

Ethan knocked on the door and waited for Cherney to make his way out of the stacks. He had a book in one hand, which he laid on the table before opening the door.

"Come in, Mr. Bosley," he said. "I'm glad you could make it. I still have that copy of *The Old Man and the Sea* that fits your client's requirements. Would you care to examine it again?"

"Yes, please," Ethan said, sitting down at the table. Cherney opened the book to the title page and waited for Ethan to look at it. Ethan checked again for the signature and the color of the dust jacket. "Very nice copy," he said.

"As I said before, we were lucky to find the olive jacket," Cherney said. "They are quite rare, you know."

"What did you say was the asking price?"

"Two thousand. It's worth every penny."

"I'm sure. You do understand that this is a cash transaction?"

"I understood that it's going into a private collection, right?"

"That's correct. My client is not in the business of selling from his collection. He was thinking that twelve hundred for a copy fitting his requirements would be a fair offer. Would you be interested at that price?"

Mr. Cherney dropped his glasses around his neck. "It's a bit under market value, and I do have another party interested."

"I see. Perhaps we could go as high as fifteen hundred. The signature is quite faded, isn't it?"

He drummed his fingers on his chin. "All right," he said. "I think I will let it go for that. Maybe we can do more business in the future as well. I have an acid-free slipcase here for the book. Do be careful about exposing the book to direct sunlight, especially with the dust jacket color being central to its value."

"Yes, of course," Ethan said. "I understand."

Cherney slid the book into the case and handed it to Ethan. "Please pay the clerk on your way out. Cash, of course, as we agreed. Please do come back. Our inventory is upgraded frequently."

"It's been a pleasure," Ethan said, then paused. "By the way, you did mention something about a Hammett, *The Maltese Falcon,* I believe. My client expressed an interest, at the right price, of course."

"Why yes. We have only recently acquired that book. It's quite rare, and this copy is impeccable."

"Perhaps I could see it before I go?"

"I'm sorry, but we keep our high-end books in a secure situation. We bring them in only when we have a serious customer. Arrangements would have to be made."

"Let me talk to my client. He would require the same anonymity, of course."

"I understand," he said. "Do call if he's interested, and we will make arrangements to bring the book forward."

On the way out, Ethan showed the slipcase to the clerk. "I'm to pay you," he said.

"Yes, Mr. Cherney just rang. He said fifteen hundred was the price."

Ethan counted out the money and tucked the case under his arm.

"Thank you for coming in," she said. "Oh, by the way, Mr. . . . ," she checked his name again, "Bosley. Mia Layla said to tell you hello next time I saw you."

"Mia?"

"The girl in the dress shop upstairs."

"Oh, yes, Mia. Tell her I said hello, won't you?"

Chapter 31

Captain Armen arrived at the camper early the next morning with a folder in his hand.

"Don't you ever sleep, Captain?" Ethan said.

"Not when someone's spending my money. You going to invite me in?"

Captain Armen sat down on the couch and placed a folder next to him.

"Black or white?" Ethan asked.

"Black."

Ethan poured the coffee and handed one to Armen. He then retrieved the Hemingway for him. "Here it is," he said, handing money back. "I negotiated for fifteen hundred."

Armen looked it over. "I don't get it," he said. "That kind of money for an old book?"

"Old *rare* book," Ethan said.

Armen sipped at his coffee. "So, did you mention to your client that you might be interested in the Hammett book?"

Ethan nodded. "Cherney's eyes lit up, but

he didn't have it at the store. They keep the high-end stuff secured somewhere. He said they could bring it in upon request."

Armen held out the appraisal that Anna had copied for him. "Have you looked at this?"

Ethan shook his head. "Once, briefly."

"Most of these books in here cost more than the Sheriff's Department has. Appears rare book dealing is more costly than drug dealing."

"From what I can tell, more addictive as well," Ethan said.

"Here's the thing, Poser, we can't be certain as to how many of these books have already shipped out or how long this scam might have been going on."

"More coffee?"

"No offense, Poser, but I've already got the tremors. There is one other thing we need to discuss."

Ethan set his cup down. "Go on."

"About this Dakota Chance guy."

"What about him?"

"I arrested him and his girlfriend yesterday."

"What? Were they stealing from the collection?"

"Dealing," he said. "I checked Chance's record. He'd been in trouble for dealing drugs in the past, so I set up a little surveillance outside the library. Hadn't been there long when this pretty gal showed up and then a line of customers. Looked like half-price sale day."

"And the girl's name?"

"Mia something or the other. Lily, I think it was."

"Layla?"

"That's it. Arrested them both."

"Damn," Ethan said. "They are in Anna's book club."

"Pretext to hang around and pick up customers, I'd guess," Armen said. "They've got plenty of time to read now."

"We're getting in pretty fast on this, Captain. You have a plan?"

"I believe it's time to tell that book dealer you are definitely interested in the Hammett. We need to keep him hooked until we have sufficient evidence to make a case. Maybe we could even track down where they secure these books. In the meantime, you could do a little detective work for the department."

"Does this mean I'm no longer under suspicion?"

"Means I'm keeping you close at hand."

"Like what kind of detective work?"

"Like Anna gets the key to Special Collections and the two of you cross-check the inventory against this appraisal. There's a hell of a lot of money behind those doors, and we need a better picture of what's going on. Stick to the higher-end stuff, so we can get a realistic estimate fast."

"And if we get caught?"

"One year in county for breaking and entering, so don't get caught. In the meantime, what can you tell me about this Morrigan guy?"

"He's smart. He's an archivist and a stickler for detail, and he's a successful fundraiser. He guards that collection with his life. No one gets in there without his approval. He's the boss, and he never lets anyone forget it. What are you getting at, Captain?"

"Cleaning his office is part of your duties, right?"

Ethan looked up through his brows at Armen. "I'm the custodian, if that's what you mean."

"You have access to the office when he's not around?"

"I clean it *only* when he's not around. Morrigan doesn't like to be disturbed. You're not asking me to—"

"Of course not. I'm the law, remember? It's just that sometimes it pays to be especially observant, that's all. There's a lot riding on this, Poser."

Captain Armen stood and gathered up his things. "There is one other thing."

"Yes?"

"Is that your dog hanging around here?"

"He's a stray. I've tried to get him to come to me, but he runs off. Why?"

"Looks half starved to me. Maybe you ought to call the dog catcher. Oh, I almost forgot. I obtained a warrant to check Morrigan's personal bank account. Funny thing, his withdrawals and Clarence Belowe's deposits are curiously similar."

***

Ethan met Anna at the doughnut shop on Sixth Street. She was wearing her exercise clothes and no makeup, revealing a small spray of freckles that he'd never noticed before. They sat at a back booth where they could talk, and he unraveled the tale that Captain Armen had presented him. She looked up from her doughnut when he told her about Morrigan's and Belowe's accounts.

"He's on Morrigan's trail for sure," Ethan said.

"I don't think he's involved, Ethan. That collection is his baby. He'd never do anything to jeopardize it. Anyway, why would he need someone like Belowe in the first place? He could just walk out with those books himself if he wanted."

"I don't know," he said. "But Armen wants Morrigan checked out. He hinted that it wouldn't hurt for a look around his office."

She narrowed her eyes at him. "Ethan, that could get us fired."

"A look around the next time I clean his office, that's all. You don't happen to know his schedule today?"

"He has a board meeting at four on Wednesdays. He usually leaves his office open and comes back after the meeting to close up."

"There is one other thing," he said.

"What?"

"Captain Armen arrested Dakota Chance and Mia Layla for selling drugs. Apparently they've been using the library as their headquarters."

"And Book Club Central, too, I suppose? My God, Ethan, drugs?"

"Turns out your intuition about their lack of interest in books was warranted." He pushed his cup aside. "OK, so here's the plan as I see it. I'm to set up another meeting with Cherney at the bookstore for a look at the Hammett and express an interest in buying. And our friend Armen suggested one more thing."

Anna leaned back in her seat. "Yet more?"

"After seeing the appraisal and the prices involved, he's concerned that something big is going down."

"He and I both," she said. "A scandal like this could shake this whole town."

"He wants us to go into Special Collections and cross-check the inventory against the appraisal."

"Ethan, I don't know if that's advisable at this point. Morrigan could be suspicious. Anyway, Captain Armen's the authority here, not us."

"The problem is, he can't do anything without alerting Morrigan. So, if we don't do it and the collection is being gutted . . . I admit it's risky, Anna, but we could be talking millions in losses, the kind of money people can get drowned for."

"I worry about going in there again," she

said. "Morrigan is no fool, and he keeps a careful eye on that collection. And if he gets suspicious . . ."

"I know," Ethan said. "But I'll worry more if we don't do it."

Chapter 32

First thing Wednesday, Ethan hid the flash drive that he'd brought with him under his cleaning supplies. Then he waited until nine o'clock before calling Hathaway's for an appointment, after which he alerted Captain Armen's office. He spent the remaining hours cleaning restrooms as usual, working his way through the floors. At three thirty that afternoon, he circled back and began cleaning Anna's office. From there he could see directly into Dr. Morrigan's office.

Dr. Morrigan sat at his desk, his glasses pulled down on his nose as he studied a sheet of paper. Ethan swept the floor in Anna's office before taking her trash out. She looked up at him as he went by but said nothing.

On his way back, he met Dr. Morrigan, who was just coming out of his office. He was carrying a briefcase and wearing a hat. He didn't speak or acknowledge Ethan as they passed.

Ethan waited until Anna gave him the

high sign that Morrigan had left the building before wheeling the supply cart into his office. He placed it between him and the window to block the view. Morrigan's office smelled of stale coffee, and his desk calendar was filled with notes written in red ink. His computer was on, its sleep light blinking hypnotically.

First, he swept the floor, then he emptied the trash before setting the can on the desk. Just in case Morrigan showed up, it would be apparent that he was in the midst of cleaning his office. He could see Anna through the window and, beyond that, Diego asleep behind a newspaper in Periodicals.

Opening the desk file drawer, he quickly thumbed through the folders, many of which were empty or filled with old, dated book orders. He searched the desk drawer—red ink pens, paper clips, rubber bands, a bottle of aspirin.

The computer blinked on, indifferent to the intrusion. He crouched below the desk, retrieved his flash drive, and slipped it into the USB port. He hit the space bar and waited as the computer hummed back to life. He looked out the office window. Anna had her back to the office and was checking out books to an old woman carrying a paper bag.

He downloaded the document file and, at the last moment, the trash file as well. Peering around the computer, he could see Anna. She was facing the office with her thumb pointing back to the entrance. He pulled the flash drive, dropped it into his pocket, and hit the sleep button.

No sooner had the computer dozed off than Morrigan came into the office. By then, Ethan was busy dust mopping the floor. Morrigan took a paper off his desk and left again without saying a word.

Ethan closed Morrigan's door and headed for the basement, taking a deep breath at the bottom of the stairs. He waited there in his shop until closing time. He made his usual rounds, checking to be certain that the library was empty and secured before exiting through the back door. The call came shortly after he got home. "Mr. Cherney has retrieved the Hammett from storage and would like for you to come in to examine the copy."

***

Ethan parked a distance from the Hathaway Building. If things went awry and he had to make a hasty departure, he didn't want his car tag identified. He headed inside. The evening was cool, a gentle breeze out of the east, smelling slightly of fall weather. He hesitated a moment outside the bookstore. Role-playing was not something he was comfortable doing, particularly with so much at stake.

The clerk at the desk looked as if she hadn't moved since the last time he was there. He cleared his throat, and she looked up from her reading.

"Excuse me," he said. "I've an appointment with Mr. Cherney, six o'clock."

"Oh, yes," she said. "He's expecting you, Mr. . . ."

"Bosley," he said. "Ross Bosley."

"Go on back. I'll let him know you have arrived."

Cherney was waiting at the door. "Come in, Mr. Bosley," he said. "Please, have a seat."

Ethan sat down at the table. He scanned the area as Cherney retrieved a chair for himself. The air was still, and silence permeated the enclosure. The space was outfitted with top-to-bottom metal bookshelves, all filled to capacity with books and slipcases. In the back was a door, oversize and weighty.

"Was your client happy with his purchase?" Cherney asked.

"He was satisfied with the condition and the authenticity of the signature," Ethan said.

"Fine, fine," he said. "And the Hammett?"

"Yes. He's asked for more detail. I'm assuming you have it available. I would need to examine it for his information."

Cherney drummed his fingers on the table. "Yes. If you will follow me, it's in the back. Would you mind wearing these archival gloves? Oil from the hands can be quite destructive, you know."

"Of course," Ethan said.

"This way, please."

They made their way through the shelves to the back. Cherney swung the door open and turned on the light, revealing a small, claustrophobic room jammed with all manner of ancient tomes, maps, and documents. A plain table sat at the back with a straight-backed chair and a lamp.

"Please," he said, pointing to the chair. "I'll get the Hammett."

Ethan slipped on the archival gloves and sat down at the desk. The room was stale and breathless. Cherney retrieved a large slipcase from the back, put on his gloves, and lay the volume in front of Ethan. The Hammett's cover had mellowed with age into a reddish-brown patina, and its corners were slightly bumped with use.

"*The Maltese Falcon,*" he said, opening the book gently, reverently. "Signed," he said, pointing to the signature. "Incredible, isn't it?"

Ethan touched the book. Even he yielded to the moment, to its existence.

"The provenance?" he asked.

"Beyond reproach," he said. "Any collector would die for this."

Ethan looked up. "And the price?"

"Twenty-five thousand."

"That's a lot of money," Ethan said.

"It's a lot of book. You'll not find it anywhere else, not at this price, and the transaction will be absolutely discreet. Your client can be assured of that."

Ethan closed the book and removed his gloves. "A purchase of this magnitude cannot be made lightly. I'm sure you understand. At some point my client will need to examine it for himself."

Cherney put the volume back into the slipcase. "It's not something I can let out. A book of this quality and condition must be examined in-house. If your client would like an appointment, I can arrange to have it brought here to the store once again for his convenience."

Ethan stood. "I will inform him, but his desire for anonymity complicates his ability to collect freely. I'm sure you understand."

"You have my number," he said. "A book of this rarity is in much demand by collectors, Mr. Bosley. I wouldn't wait too long. We also have a contact on the *Principia,* just for your information."

On Ethan's way out of the store, the clerk looked up and smiled. "Oh, I wanted to ask you something," she said.

"Yes, what is it?"

"I was wondering if you'd seen Mia lately?"

"No, I haven't."

"She hasn't been back to work, you see. We often ate lunch together at the coffee shop, but I haven't seen her for several days. Her boss doesn't know where she is either. I was concerned that something may have happened to her."

"I'm sorry I can't be of help," he said.

"If you see her, tell her to come by."

"Yes, I will."

"Have a good day," she said, turning back to her book.

Chapter 33

Come in, Ethan," Anna said. "I've been worried about you."

"I'm officially in the rare book business," he said.

"You've been to see Cherney?"

"Indeed. And I had a firsthand look at the Hammett too. I'm on the hook for talking to my client about buying it. He says I have to bring him into the store to examine the copy."

"How is that going to work?"

"I don't know. Do you have a spare twenty-five thousand lying around? I guess I can always tell him that my client has decided against the purchase. This guy is running a hell of a business, Anna, and he's no fool."

"So," she said, "did you find anything in Morrigan's office that will help? My heart nearly stopped when he walked in the front door."

Ethan reached into his pocket and took out the flash drive. "Fire up your computer, and we'll find out."

For an hour they searched through the documents, coming up with nothing but library purchase orders, various correspondence to the State Department, and an occasional inter-office memorandum.

"That's it," he said. "Nothing. And what was left of the paper files were dated and obsolete. My guess is he's not using them at all anymore."

"Maybe we have it all wrong, Ethan. Maybe he knows nothing about any of this."

Ethan leaned back in his chair. "Or maybe he has the important records in Special Collections under lock and key. But," he said, hesitating, "there is one file we haven't looked in yet."

"What's that?"

"Trash," he said, clicking on the icon. "I downloaded this as an afterthought. Sometimes people forget what they've dumped in these things."

He scrolled down through the files, looking for anything that might give them a lead. He was nearly at the bottom when he spotted a file that was addressed to "Morgon," rather than to Dr. Morrigan. He opened the file.

I know what is happening on the mezzanine on third. Bring ten thousand dollars cash to the park lake pier tonight, and you will never hear from me again. C.B.

"That's it," Ethan said, looking up at Anna. "And check the date of the email. It's the same time frame as Clarence Belowe's death."

Anna sat down, her hand over her mouth. "My God, Belowe was blackmailing Dr. Morrigan."

"Morrigan is selling off the rare books to Cherney," Ethan said. "Clarence must have picked up on it. Apparently he got a little too greedy with his demands."

Anna shuddered. "Morrigan murdered Belowe?"

The knock on the door startled them both. "You expecting anyone?" Ethan asked.

Anna shook her head. "It's late, Ethan. Who would come at this hour?"

Anna opened the door to see Captain Armen standing there. "I'm looking for Ethan," he said. "Saw his car. Mind if I come in?"

"He's here. Come in," Anna said.

"Ethan," Armen said, "you have any news for me?"

"Cherney had the Hammett. My client will

have to come in to examine it. I told him I'd let him know. But we have a small problem with that, Captain. I don't have a client, and I don't have the money."

"Maybe we can stall him on that," he said.

"That's not all," Ethan said, pulling up the trash file on the computer. "We just found this on Morrigan's computer. A little surprise."

Armen read Belowe's note and pushed his hat back. "I'll be damned," he said. "Looks like Clarence Belowe blackmailed the wrong guy."

"Is Dr. Morrigan going to be arrested?" Anna asked.

"First, we need to know how deep this goes," Armen said. "Is Morrigan selling to others or just Cherney, and if so, who? Can we track them down? I want the net cast wide while we can."

Ethan said, "So what do we do about the Hammett? Cherney is going to want to move the deal, and it's always possible the book could be put back into Special Collections if we wait too long."

"You folks have an idea of someone who could go in as *the* client and stall this guy for a bit?"

Ethan said, "I told Cherney my client

preferred to remain anonymous, that I wasn't certain he would want to come in. The thing is, Captain, the rare book business is a lot more complex than most people realize. We can't just send anyone in. Anna educated me enough to get by, but, believe me, Cherney could pick up on a mistake."

"All right," he said. "We need to move fast on this. One of the things we have to know is just how big the operation is. The best way to find that out is to determine how much has been pilfered out of that collection already. The law can't do that without a warrant, which could blow the whole thing up. That leaves you two to go in."

Ethan said, "You do understand that Dr. Morrigan may have killed one person already?"

"As I indicated, we don't need every book checked to make an arrest," Armen said. "It's pretty obvious that they are concentrating mostly on the high-dollar stuff, so keep your search to that. It will save time."

Anna said, "You understand that Ethan and I have to go to work tomorrow knowing that we might be in danger from our own boss?"

Captain Armen put on his hat and made his way to the door. "Most of us will, when you think about it," he said.

Chapter 34

After Armen left, Ethan and Anna stayed up late talking about Morrigan and the collection and the death of Clarence Belowe. They talked about the dilemma they now found themselves in and how they must enter the Special Collections room once again. They concluded that Captain Armen was right, that the first thing was to know the extent of damage to the collection and then they could determine how wide and extensive the theft ring was.

The plan would be to meet in the parking lot at two a.m. the following night, enter the Special Collections as they had before, and take a more complete account of the higher-end books.

They talked on into the night, sharing personal feelings that neither had shared before, taking comfort in each other and in the moment. Anna fell asleep next to him. He covered her then, gently moving her hair away from her face. Once he was certain that she slept soundly, he drove home, on a whim swinging past the park lake pier. The moon shimmered on the water, peaceful and silent.

He wondered there in the quiet of the night at the contradictions of a man such as Morrigan, someone who had dedicated his life to the preservation and care of ancient treasures, then to rise up and kill another human, leaving him in the cold waters of the park lake.

***

At work the next morning, Ethan waited in his car until opening time. The events had coalesced faster than he could process them. The death of a man, the stress and fear they'd all experienced, had precipitated from the craving of the humans for the ancient scribblings of their ancestors. It was inexplicable, really, and now the library, normally a safe haven, had become a potential crime scene.

To make matters worse, the crime itself might well have been executed by the man in charge of it all, the one who had nourished and built the collection itself. It was possible that this same man had killed Clarence Belowe and defiled the sanctity of Special Collections for his own gain. Ethan felt betrayed.

At exactly eight thirty, he started his daily routine. Anna arrived shortly, followed by Dr. Morrigan, with his usual coffee in hand. Soon Diego had taken his place in Periodicals and was dozing behind a newspaper.

The day passed without event, and by late afternoon, Ethan had worked his way up to the mezzanine. He walked his dust mop from wall to wall while studying the door of Special Collections. Behind it lay the secrets of the past, but for all he knew, those coveted tomes may already be in the hands of unknown collectors. Could Morrigan have been so cold as to deceive those who had trusted him with their irreplaceable treasures?

At four thirty, he went downstairs. Anna was talking to someone at the checkout desk, a man. He handed her something, then left. Ethan went to the basement to wait until closing time. When he climbed the stairs to the ground floor that evening, Anna was gone, as was Morrigan, their offices dark. He set the security alarm and exited through the back door to his car. That night, he'd return for a different kind of mission, one that paid even less than custodial work and was far more dangerous.

***

The town was quiet at two in the morning, the library parking lot empty. He left the car at the far end where the trees blocked the view. He'd only just shut off his lights when she pulled in next to him. She emerged wearing sweats and carrying a manila folder. A flashlight protruded from her pocket.

 She took his arm. "I feel like a cat burglar," she said, whispering.

 "You got the key to Special Collections?"

 "As soon as Dr. Morrigan left," she said, handing it to him. "And a copy of the appraisal."

 "Well, at least we don't have to climb to the third floor on the outside of the building like most cat burglars. Come on, let's get this done."

 Ethan unlocked the back door to the library and shut down the alarm system. He waited for Anna to close the door, then rechecked it to make certain it was secure. They stood in the quiet as their eyes adjusted to the darkness. She moved in close to him, and he could feel her trembling.

"No flashlight until we get to Special Collections," he said. "The blackout shades will cover us there."

"But how are we going to see in the meantime?" she asked.

"There's an exit light on third. It's enough. I could climb these stairs blindfolded, believe me."

They edged their way up the stairs to the third floor. Anna followed close to him, her hand on his arm, and soon they stood at the door of Special Collections. They paused a moment to listen before he slipped in the key and released the lock. Anna gripped his arm as the door swung open. Slivers of moonlight seeped from around the edges of the blackout shades.

He reset the lock bolt behind them and turned to her. "You can use the flashlight now." She clicked on the light, the beam slicing through the blackness. "So, where do we start?" he asked.

"Armen said keep to the most valuable books. They are stored in the back where the Hammett was."

"How do we ever find what we need in here?"

"It's called the Dewey Decimal System, Ethan. They are on the appraisal sheet as well."

"I'm glad you're a librarian. I never did understand that Dewey thing. Lead the way."

He followed her as she made her way through the shelves. "Here we are. Most are shelved vertically, just like regular books, unless they are too large, in which case they lie flat on the shelf. The more valuable ones will be in slipcases."

"Anna?"

"What?"

"Did you remember to bring your library card?"

She bumped him with her shoulder. "Will you stop."

Ethan held the flashlight while Anna checked the books against the appraisal list. When she'd reached the bottom shelf, she sat down on the floor, crossing her legs and hooking her chin in her hands.

She looked up at him. "My God, Ethan, there are dozens of missing books, including Newton's *Philosophiae naturalis principia mathematica.* It's irreplaceable and vastly expensive. The Geneva Bible is gone too."

"Are you sure?"

"They've replaced many of them with reader copies so no one would notice. Who knows how many? The whole collection is gutted. Luckily they left Jefferson's *Laws of the United States*. Probably too difficult to cover its absence."

Click.

Ethan doused the flashlight, and heat rose in his ears. At first the sound didn't register, but then he realized: Someone was unlocking the Special Collections door. He dropped down next to Anna.

"Someone is here," he said, whispering.

They slid back to the end of the shelves. Ethan's hands were damp, and his heart thumped in his chest. They'd been caught, and there was no way to escape. He could hear the squeak of the door as it opened and footsteps making their way across the room. Suddenly, the light came on. Ethan could see Dr. Morrigan scanning a shelf. He took a book, shut off the light, and went out again.

They waited in the darkness until they heard the bolt lock slide home.

Ethan leaned back. "Too close," he said. "Way too close."

"What do you suppose he was doing here, Ethan?"

"The same as us," he said. "Looking for books."

***

Captain Armen was waiting outside Anna's bungalow when they got back. He followed them in.

Ethan said, "We are lucky to be here, Captain. Morrigan came into Special Collections while we were in there, took a book, and left again."

"You sure he didn't see you?"

"I don't think he did."

Armen said, "It's really that easy? Walk in and walk out with a book, and no one knows the difference?"

Ethan shrugged. "If you're the man, it is."

Armen looked at Anna, who had said nothing since their return. "What did you find out about the inventory?"

Anna handed him the appraisal sheet. "The circled ones are those missing."

He looked it over. "All of these are gone?"

She nodded. "Maybe more. This must have been going on for a long while. Many of those books are extremely rare. The reputation of the foundation will be destroyed when all this is made public."

"We don't want it to come out just yet," Armen said. "I want the goods on these guys, all of them. Clearly Morrigan is the kingpin, the guy with the supply, but where the hell are these books going?" He looked over the appraisal again. "Is the rare book world really that damn greedy?"

"You have to understand what drives them," Anna said. "These are not just books to be read. Any given copy might be the one a collector has been searching for his whole life, that final special book that completes his collection. In many instances, it's not even about money. It's about fulfillment. It's what they live for.

"The bottom line is that collectors, even institutions themselves, are sometimes willing to look the other way to get what they want. For many, it is not a crime but the conclusion to a noble effort. That's the thinking that can go into it, and it isn't always rational."

"I'm familiar with irrational thinking," Armen said. "But this takes the prize. Why is the Hammett book not sold off? Half the collection is missing."

Anna said, "They were no doubt waiting for the right customer, the one with fire in the belly and money in hand. My guess is that they are careful about who they sell to, and that's how they've gotten away with it for so long."

She crossed her arms. "Something came up at the library today, and it gave me an idea."

"Go on," Armen said.

"A man came in and wanted to see Dr. Morrigan, who was not there at the time. I asked if I could help him. Turns out he is a lifelong collector of Americana and was completing his estate trust. He was interested in perhaps donating his books to Special Collections. He said he wanted to keep the collection together and had heard about the foundation. He said that he would come back and talk to Dr. Morrigan. He struck me as someone who cared deeply about the material, and I'm wondering if he might help us."

Armen walked to the door and turned. "Find out and let me know," he said.

Chapter 35

The next morning, Anna checked the man's card information again, a Jason Hanover. She called and arranged to meet him at the Reston Hotel for dinner. Ethan picked her up at six, finding her clad in a stunning evening dress and high-heeled shoes, her hair gathered in a sophisticated bun.

"Wow," he said, opening the car door for her. "You could convince me of anything."

"Don't start, Ethan," she said, fanning out her dress. "I've had this old thing forever."

Ethan started the car and looked over at her. "So, what's to keep this guy from going to Morrigan and sharing the plan? He doesn't know us at all."

"I thought about that," Anna said. "I'm going to tell him that Captain Armen from the Sheriff's Department suggested it and that he's welcome to call him if he has any doubts."

The hotel was one of the oldest in town, but elegant, with its twin towers, a red tile roof, and a row of matching dormer windows running its length. A concrete parking garage had been added to one end, where Ethan found the last parking space on the third level and wheeled in. They took the garage elevator down to the lobby area, where the restaurant was located.

Jason Hanover, an unassuming figure with a gray beard and flesh-colored glasses, was waiting for them at the door. Overweight, he'd fastened only the top button of his sports jacket, which fanned the tails outward like wings.

"Mr. Hanover," Anna said, "I'd like for you to meet Ethan Poser from our library staff."

Hanover adjusted his tie and reached for Ethan's hand. "Mr. Poser," he said. "Nice to meet you."

"I know this is a bit unusual," Anna said. "But we needed to talk with you before you met with Dr. Morrigan."

"I see," he said. "Well, I welcome the company. I'm in town alone, you see. I'm afraid my wife doesn't share my love of Americana. I've gone ahead and arranged for a table. I hope you don't mind?"

"Not at all," Anna said. "Lead the way."

They followed him into the restaurant, taking their places at a table near the window that overlooked Main. Cocktails were ordered, and when the waiter had gathered up their menus, Ethan said, "So, I understand you are a collector of rare books, Mr. Hanover?"

Hanover took a sip of his martini and twirled the olive on its toothpick. "That hardly describes my enthusiasm, Mr. Poser. I admit to being a quite rabid collector of Americana. While books constitute my primary interest, I also collect pertinent manuscripts and correspondence. I've even been known to pick up an occasional artifact or antique as well. It started innocently enough as a hobby, but I'm afraid it has devolved into a serious obsession."

"And where are you from?" Ethan asked.

"California. Los Angeles. I'm a real estate developer there. It has worked out well for me over the years."

Anna said, "And as I understand it, you are interested in donating your collection to our library."

"Yes, I'm determined that the collection remain intact. I've spent a lifetime putting it together, you see."

"You are still a young man, Mr. Hanover. Why would you want to give your collection away now?"

He looked over at Anna and smiled. "I don't want to spoil the evening, but frankly, it's because I'm dying."

Anna glanced at Ethan. "Oh, my. Did you say—"

"Yes," he said. "I have advanced pancreatic cancer. The prognosis is poor."

"Oh, dear," Anna said. "I'm so sorry to hear that, Mr. Hanover."

"As was I, as you might suspect. I've spent my entire life putting this collection together. It's been carefully researched and acquired, and at no small expense. But, at the same time, it's been one of the most important loves of my life. There are books in this compilation that exist nowhere else in the world. As a complete collection, it's unparalleled. I'm going to do everything I can to see that it stays that way after I'm gone.

"You see, while I may have to leave this world, my collection does not. I know this sounds odd, but that collection *is* my immortality. I don't want it to be pieced out and sold like some weekend garage sale. It includes some of the finest rare books assembled in America. I want the collection preserved, and I'm willing to do what it takes to make that happen. Your foundation has a reputation of being one of the best in the country, and that's where I want my books to be."

"Tell me," Ethan said, "how do you explain this unusual passion you have? Seems an odd thing for a real estate developer."

Hanover took a drink and studied his glass. "I'm not sure I *can* explain it. I guess it's the hunt, or perhaps the find itself, that rush of adrenaline when something you have pursued the world over is at last in your hands. Maybe it's some Freudian complex, a lingering maladjustment from childhood, though I have not thought of my life that way. Whatever it is, collecting has given me some of the most satisfying moments in my life. Now, a victim of my circumstances, my passion promises to render as much pain as pleasure."

Their dinners came, and the table fell quiet as the waiter set out his tray. Once the dishes had been served and the waiter had gone with a polite "Enjoy," Hanover cleared his throat.

"Now, permit *me* to ask *you* a question," Hanover said.

Anna nodded. "Certainly."

"Are you here representing the library's Special Collections? I mean, are you prepared to discuss the terms for the foundation's acquisition? Is that why we are here?"

"Not exactly, Mr. Hanover," Anna said. "The truth is we are here to solicit *your* help."

"I don't understand."

"We are here at the behest of Captain Armen of the Sheriff's Department. Unfortunately, Special Collections has been the victim of book theft. We thought you might be of assistance."

Hanover laid down his fork. "Theft? Your facility is not secure?"

Ethan said, "There's a fair chance that it's an inside job, which makes the collection extremely vulnerable. We believe that someone is taking the books and fencing them through a rare book store here in town. A number of volumes are missing, most of them quite valuable, as you know."

Hanover looked at Ethan, then at Anna. "And so this is all about the one person who is *not* here, I'm assuming?"

"Yes," Anna said. "Dr. Morrigan is a suspect, and he is not aware of the ongoing investigation. You see, there has also been a death that might be related, one Clarence Belowe, an ex-employee of the library, a custodian to be exact. We think it might have been the consequence of a blackmail situation."

"Dr. Morrigan again?" Hanover said.

She nodded. "We think it's possible."

"What could you want from me? I'm only a collector."

"A collector of some repute," Ethan said. "And that's exactly what we need. Let me explain."

For the next hour, Ethan set out the situation, how he had gone to the bookstore pretending to be the agent for a client and how they had purchased books, and how they had been offered the Hammett on condition that the book remain in-house until a deal was reached.

"Which means you are short a *real* client?"

"Exactly."

"And you want me to pretend to be that client?"

Ethan nodded. "I'll be with you the entire time."

"And exactly what is your job at the library, Mr. Poser?"

"I'm the replacement custodian."

He looked at Ethan. "Of course you are. Look, to think someone is stealing those books is infuriating. My collection could have easily been victimized as well."

Ethan said, "If we can expose these people now, we might have a chance at recovering those books. We want to know where they are. Who bought them. In short, we want to do everything we can to keep this collection safe, now and in the future. To do that, we need to be on the inside. A man with your experience and knowledge of rare books could go a long way in helping us stay engaged with them."

"Will you consider helping us?" Anna asked.

Ethan said, "There is one thing you need to understand first, Mr. Hanover. It could be dangerous. There's been one death already."

Mr. Hanover finished off his martini and studied them before speaking. "Given my prognosis, there's not much left for me to fear in this world," he said. "And it would give me satisfaction to help bring these people to justice."

Captain Armen's patrol car was parked next to Ethan's car when they left the hotel.

Ethan approached and waited for the captain to roll down his window. "Have you been following us?" he asked.

"Of course," Armen said. "What did you find out?"

"Hanover has agreed to go in with me as my client at the bookstore. He's been a collector a long time and knows his business. I think he's our best chance."

"He can be trusted?"

"I don't know," Ethan said. "We've been acquainted all of a couple hours at this point."

"So, what's the next move?"

"I'm going to call the bookstore, tell them I'm bringing my client in for a look at the Hammett. We'll see how it goes from there."

***

By the following day, Ethan had made his phone call to Cherney. They'd agreed to meet at six like before, that Ethan would have his client with him, and that the Hammett book would be there for his examination.

At five thirty, Ethan picked up Jason Hanover from the hotel, and they drove to Hathaway's Used and Rare Books.

The clerk smiled. "Mr. Bosley," she said. "Mr. Cherney is expecting you. Please go on back."

"I've somehow missed this store in my wanderings," Hanover said. "It's quite interesting, isn't it?"

Ethan introduced Hanover to Cherney, emphasizing the need for anonymity, to which Cherney readily agreed. He disappeared into the vault, returning with the copy of *The Maltese Falcon,* and laid it out on the table in front of Hanover.

"1930?" Hanover asked.

"Yes." Cherney said. "First edition."

"Of the book itself," Hanover said. "The story was first serialized in *Black Mask Magazine* 1929, as I'm sure you know."

"Indeed," Cherney said.

Hanover slipped on the archival gloves and opened the book. "It's signed," he said. "Do we know if it's authentic?"

"Verified," Cherney said. "And it's a first printing, first issue. The condition is fine, as you can see."

"The corner is slightly bumped," he said.

"Barely noticeable," Cherney said. "Any collector would be proud to own this copy."

"What is the book priced?"

"For a cash transaction, twenty-two thousand. I understand you have a rather large collection, Mr. Hanover?"

"Extensive," he said. "Americana for the most, though I do dabble with some incunable, mostly for investment purposes."

"Do you think you might be interested in the Hammett? I also have other books I could make available."

"I'm rather taken with this copy," Hanover said. "But I never make a purchase without a little research. Do you have any provenance available?"

"I'm afraid not," Cherney said.

"What else do you have that I might be interested in purchasing?"

"We sell all over the world, Mr. Hanover, to individuals as well as museums, and we have some of the rarest and most exquisite copies that can be found anywhere. For example, we currently have an extraordinary copy of Newton's *Philosophiae naturalis principia mathematica,* the 1729 English translation. It is an impeccable copy."

"Really?" Hanover said, glancing at Ethan. "And it is available to be seen?"

"We would have to retrieve it from our warehouse, which is climate controlled and secured, of course. You can understand the need?"

"And if I were interested in both the *Principia* and the Hammett?"

"I think we could make you a rather nice deal, Mr. Hanover. It's my understanding that your collection is a private one. Is that correct?"

"I'm not associated with any institution or foundation. This collection has been a personal endeavor," Hanover said, standing. "I'll be in touch. Good day, Mr. Cherney. Your store is quite inviting."

***

They sat in the car in front of Hanover's hotel.

Ethan turned to him. "What Cherney said about Newton's *Principia.* I saw your eyes light up."

"It's very rare and very expensive," Hanover said. "I've never seen one in all my years collecting."

"And what do you make of the secure storage story?"

"My guess is that it's true. That sort of material has to be carefully handled."

"What kind of money are we talking about, for the *Principia,* I mean?"

"Market value is somewhere around eight

hundred thousand to a million, depending on condition," he said.

"It just so happens that Special Collections is missing one," Ethan said. "Are you going to be in town a while, Mr. Hanover?"

Hanover got out of the car and leaned back in. "Wouldn't miss seeing that book for the world," he said.

Chapter 36

The situation at work had become increasingly stressful for Anna. Every time she encountered Dr. Morrigan, passed him in the hallway, or had to visit his office, her pulse peaked with anxiety. She'd thought she'd known him so well, a man dedicated to his work, rigid but competent. He had always been difficult, a perfectionist, but was committed to his profession and driven by his love of rare books. Now what she saw was a man who had violated the very code by which he'd lived, and it pained her deeply.

Ethan and Book Club Central had been her lifeline throughout this whole catastrophe. Members of the club had shown her repeatedly that what appeared to be a group of ordinary people was in fact a gathering of warm and intelligent friends. Sharing with each other through their book discussions had been both gratifying and enlightening.

And as for Ethan, she had known from the beginning that his intellect and curiosity would not long abide the routine of custodial work. There was in him an inquisitiveness that needed feeding, and she had seen his disquiet increase over the weeks. Such curiosity was both his strength and his weakness and could easily place him at risk.

***

Before getting in her car, she checked her phone and found a text message from Ethan. Could she come to his camper? They needed to talk. Certain that he had news about the books, she drove straight there. His car was parked in front of the camper.

Ethan, still buttoning his shirt, opened the door. "I wasn't sure you received my message, Anna. Come on in."

She took a seat at the table, and he sat down across from her. She thought he looked tired. Maybe she was not the only one feeling the stress of the situation.

"How did it go?" she asked.

"Hanover and I met with Cherney as planned. Hanover was convincing, calm, and informed. Cherney smelled another possible deal, and Hanover brought him along nicely."

"What book?"

"The *Principia*."

Anna pushed back from the table. "You're kidding."

"So, Hanover doesn't even flinch. He asks to see it, but they don't have it on hand. They will have to retrieve it from their specially equipped storage. Can they arrange to meet again? So Hanover agrees, but he's quite busy at the moment, and he will let them know when. The guy was cool as ice, I'm telling you.

"Here's what I'm thinking, and Hanover agrees. This warehouse he's talking about could be where they're keeping the really high-end stuff stolen from Special Collections and who knows where else. It's climate controlled, which is what they need to maintain their condition, and they can be retrieved at their convenience and sold with discretion. If someone at some point detects missing copies from Special Collections, who's to know when they were taken or where they are. They aren't likely to be served a warrant and raided by the police, because nobody knows where they are."

Anna fell quiet as she thought through what he'd just said. "Ethan, if only we knew where."

"Exactly," he said. "That's the solution, isn't it, but Cherney is damn well not saying. Here's what I'm thinking, Anna. Suppose we set up a time to view this *Principia.* We have someone, Captain Armen, for example, watch the store and tail them to the warehouse. The good captain can obtain a search warrant, and bingo, we've got Cherney *and* the books in one easy bust."

"Sounds easy, but remember that these are not your common criminal types. They are sophisticated, clever people, and they clearly know how to work the system. You would need to be careful, extremely careful."

***

Ethan answered the knock at the door. "Come on in, Captain," he said.

Armen slid in next to Anna at the table. For the next ten minutes Ethan laid out what had gone down at the bookstore and the details about the warehouse.

Armen said, "A warehouse? You think they have a warehouse with these stolen books stored in it?"

"That's what Cherney implied. Why couldn't

we set up a time for Jason Hanover and me to examine the *Principia* at the bookstore? Cherney or someone would have to make a trip to the warehouse at some point both before and after the meeting. If any book would need special storage, it would be the *Principia*. I'm thinking that's for sure where they'd keep it."

"And we could tail him when he goes," he said. "You think this Hanover guy can pull it off?"

Ethan smiled. "He had Cherney counting his money by the time we left. In fact, I was thinking he might have done this sort of transaction before himself."

Captain Armen stood to leave. "Sounds like a plan—get in touch with Cherney and seal the deal. Set up a time to go see the . . . what the hell did you call it?"

"Isaac Newton's *Principia*," Anna said.

"Yeah, that one. What was the price again?"

"Eight hundred thousand to a million, depending on the day."

"Holy Isaac Newton," he said. "Don't let anything happen to that book, Poser, or we are all going to prison."

Chapter 37

On the way to work the next morning, Ethan purposely drove by the school where he'd taught. The bell had just rung, and kids were funnelling from the schoolyard back into the building. The morning was alive with laughter and teasing. There were times he missed the human interaction that flourished in the school environment. He missed it most often while in the quiet slog of custodial duties.

After opening up the library, he fixed himself his usual cup of coffee. There was a lot on the line for the day. One mistake, and they could be in serious jeopardy. He thought about Jason Hanover, such an avid collector, a man of advancing age and a bleak future. Here was a guy of obvious wealth who could have had anything he wanted, but what he wanted most in life was to keep his collection together. Something about that kind of passion defied explanation. Love, greed, and power, man's usual irrational motives, failed to explain Hanover's fervor for rare books. Even as he approached the end of his life, it was his collection that concerned him the most.

Diego knocked on the door once before coming in and sitting down at Ethan's desk.

"Hey, *amigo*," he said. "Are you sleeping in the library again?"

"You are here early this morning, Diego."

"We are having our book club meeting soon," he said. "I must be prepared. Many ask for my ideas."

"Who's up?" Ethan asked.

"Imani Bell," he said. "She has chosen *The Invisible Man* by Ralph Ellison. It's a big book, very important book."

"Great choice," Ethan said. "Have you read it?'

"Oh, *sí*, I am nearly done. It's a very good book."

Ethan looked at the time. "I need to get to work, Diego. There's a banana in my lunch sack."

"I now eat green bananas too much," he said. "I think you are in need of a wife. Maybe you could do me a favor, Ethan?"

"You can't smoke in here, Diego."

"This is for Imani. She asked me to see

if I could get a recording of her book *The Invisible Man.* She is having much trouble finding it. I think she doesn't read so well. I told her I would ask you, and you could ask Anna to find one."

"Ah, I see," he said. "I think that can be arranged. I'll leave it on my desk for you."

"I think for sure she doesn't want anyone to know," he said.

"It's our secret, Diego. I will talk to you later."

***

At lunch, Ethan made his call to Jason Hanover at the hotel.

"I'd like to come over after work," he said. "We need to arrange for a meeting on the *Principia.*"

"Yes, of course," Hanover said. "I wonder if you might bring Anna as well. There are some things I would like to discuss concerning the future of my collection."

"I'll check with her," Ethan said. "About six, then?"

"Room twenty-three," he said.

***

Anna met Ethan in the library parking lot. He opened the door, and she slid in. She smelled of jasmine, and her hair lit up in the late sunlight. Ethan pulled out and turned onto Main.

"Do you think Hanover is still interested in leaving his collection with us after all that's happened?" she asked.

"Maybe he figures everything that could go wrong has already."

Anna looked out her window. She was wearing turquoise earrings and a matching necklace that lay rich and luscious against her pearl skin.

"The uncertainty of what's happening to that collection is stressing me," she said. "What's to keep these guys from just disappearing and leaving us to deal with it?"

"The *Principia,* for one," he said. "And there's still plenty of money to be made to just walk away."

"And there's something else we haven't talked about," she said. "Something that's been worrying me."

He glanced at her, her profile struck against the waning light. "Yes?"

"You see, there are other documents in Special Collections that are just as rare and valuable as the books. For example, we have rare maps, memorabilia, autographs, correspondence from famous people. Here's the problem, Ethan: those can be sold separately, and often for more money."

"You mean they can be removed from the original documents?"

"Exactly. And then sold separately. Many of them would be impossible to trace. To complicate matters, the process of splitting them could diminish much of the value of the original document."

"And you think that might be happening?"

"I don't know for certain, but why wouldn't it be? Look, no one understands the market for these things better than Morrigan. If he would sell our rarest books, why would he hesitate to destroy others to make an even larger profit? The point is that he has to be shut down soon, or there might be nothing left to save."

Ethan pulled into the Reston Hotel parking garage and shut off the engine. "Before we go in, Diego stopped by this morning. He asked that I talk to you about something."

"Oh?"

"He said that Imani Bell had made her selection for Book Club Central."

"*The Invisible Man,*" she said. "A great choice."

"He said that she had some difficulty reading and would I ask you for an audio recording of the book for her."

"Imani already has a copy of the book. I checked it out to her myself."

"It might not be for Imani, you see."

She looked over at him. "There are some sources I can check."

"He asked that we not let on to anyone because Imani might be embarrassed. Could you leave it on my desk? I will see he gets it."

She smiled. "I'll check on it."

"Thanks. Ready to go in?"

"You know, Ethan, we're depending pretty heavily on this Hanover guy. I mean, we barely know him. If he blows this, the whole thing could fall apart."

"We've little choice at this point. Look, once we know where that warehouse is, we will have these guys right where we want them."

"I do hope you're right," she said. "Our jobs depend on it, maybe our lives."

Chapter 38

Jason Hanover answered the door. He was pale, and dark circles underscored his eyes. He'd offset a button on his shirt, which had pushed his collar up under his ear, making one shoulder look higher than the other.

"Come in," he said, stepping aside. "Could I offer you something to drink?"

Ethan shook his head. "Thanks, we're fine."

Hanover took his handkerchief out of his pocket and dabbed at his upper lip. "Sorry about this," he said. "Chemo hangover. Never know when it's going to hit."

"Is there anything we can do for you?" Anna asked.

He pursed his lips. "It passes. They say it's rat poison, you know. Sometimes I'm not sure it's worth it."

"We're moving ahead with Cherney's offer for a look at the *Principia*," Ethan said. "I've talked to Captain Armen, who plans to put a tail on Cherney as soon as we have a date set to examine the book. I wanted to clear it with you."

"Now, what is it exactly you will need from me?" he asked.

"We make contact with Cherney. Tell him we want a look at this Newton book, that we are seriously interested in a deal. And then we wait. Captain Armen will stake him out and follow him to the warehouse. Once he has a location, he can obtain a search warrant. With luck, we'll be able to recover something. Maybe we can locate a few of Cherney's other customers as well."

"You up to it?" Anna asked Hanover.

He rubbed at his face as he thought for a moment. "Make it Monday at six. I should be finished with some business I need to complete by then. I'm having my collection appraised and inventoried for tax purposes. The whole thing has been quite stressful."

He sat down on the end of the bed, crossing his arms over his chest. "Which brings me to why I asked Anna to come."

Anna threw a quick glance at Ethan. "You are uncertain about donating to our collection with all that's going on?" she asked.

"I was uncertain. I'm sure you can understand. Dr. Morrigan's reputation as an archivist was one of the main reasons for wanting in to the collection in the first place. He is known nationwide for his knowledge of rare books, but now this . . .

"The thing is, I have already made many of the arrangements, had my trust brought up, and selected my business successor for my upcoming retirement. Not having a safe home for my collection was a complication, of course."

"Look," Anna said, "this has all come about because of one guy's betrayal. With him brought to justice and the collection restored, there's no reason it couldn't be perfectly safe for your books. If we were to get this resolved, maybe you would reconsider? If you don't mind me asking, Mr. Hanover, what might be the approximate value of your collection?"

Hanover looked at his hands, threading his fingers together as he thought it over.

"This may not make much sense to you, or anyone other than a dedicated collector, but I've rarely thought about it in that way. It's never been about money for me. To tell you the truth, this is the first official appraisal I have had done.

"I had this goal, you see. That's what I thought about, reaching this goal. That's what

I wanted to accomplish more than anything." He got up and walked to the window, where he looked down on the street. He lowered his head and was quiet for a moment. He turned to Anna and said, "Millions, I suppose. There's no better collection of Americana in the country."

Anna lifted her brows. "That's quite remarkable, Mr. Hanover, and all while running a successful business."

"Ironic," he said. "I ran the business to buy the books. It began slowly, you see. Like most people, I started out with the inexpensive stuff, modern firsts mostly, gambling on an unknown author becoming well known—a risky endeavor to be sure, but you haven't invested much either. And then I moved into Americana, history and the like, and then finally into the very rare and expensive items.

"First thing I know, I'm totally and hopelessly addicted. I can't really explain it. The acquisition of what I needed, wanted, was my reason for living. The money was always secondary—necessary, of course, to fund my collecting, but never a goal in itself. If I found the book I wanted, I managed somehow to come up with the money to buy it. There was always a house to sell somewhere, a deal to be made—thus the success of what would otherwise have been a rather ordinary business."

"And now to have to give the collection away?" Ethan said.

"We all give it away in the end, don't we?" he said. "It was the hunt, the acquisition, and the finishing of what was sometimes said to be impossible to finish."

He turned his attention to Anna. "The thing is, addiction makes a person vulnerable. Over the years, I've paid more than I should have, taken money from the business when I couldn't afford it, shorted those who depended on me in order to get what I wanted. I've exploited and been exploited. You see, the irony here is that I can understand better than I should how someone can go too far."

"Such a collection as yours is truly outstanding," she said.

"You're willing to go through with this, then?" Ethan asked.

"I could never miss an opportunity to see the *Principia,* and I wanted to share something with you and Anna now. I've made the decision to leave my collection to your library despite the current situation. It's all about people, in the end. I'm convinced it will be safe in your care."

Chapter 39

Diego showed up at the library Monday and took up a study carrel in the back with his audio of *The Invisible Man* that Anna had managed to get for him. Ethan had nearly forgotten that Book Club Central would be meeting at the end of the day. He made a mental note to keep the Genealogy Room unlocked for the meeting.

First chance, he called Hathaway's bookstore and confirmed the appointment for six, after which he contacted Captain Armen to let him know that everything was go as planned. Armen confirmed his plan to surveil the store and assured Ethan that he'd done that sort of thing many times and that he was not to worry about that end of the strategy.

Then Ethan rang up Jason Hanover at his hotel. "It's on, Mr. Hanover," he said. "I'll pick you up at five thirty. That will give us time to get to the bookstore. Don't forget that my name is Ross Bosley, not Poser. My job will be to look confident. Your job is to convince

Cherney that you cannot leave town without that book in hand."

"I've spent my life convincing book dealers," he said. "I must admit a certain excitement about all this. I suppose it's the possibility of actually seeing the *Principia*. Do you have any notion how rare that volume is, Poser? It's the equivalent of seeing a dinosaur walking down the street."

"I know what it costs," he said. "That's enough excitement for me."

He was on his way to the second floor when Dr. Morrigan motioned him over to his office. Ethan's ears went hot.

"Yes, sir?" he said.

"Someone dumped coffee in the book drop."

"I'll see to it."

"And there are empty beer cans in the parking lot."

"Teenagers," Ethan said. "I'll pick them up."

Ethan turned to leave when Morrigan said, "That Mexican fellow who comes in here?"

"Diego Pinto?"

"Yeah, that one. He's here every day. Does he have business in the library?"

"I believe he is a member of Book Club Central. I understand he's a big reader."

"Well," he said, "I'll be working quite late tonight. Leave the back alarm off. I'll set it myself when I'm finished."

Ethan took a deep breath and went to find Anna, who was shelving books in Nonfiction.

"Hi," he said.

She looked up and smiled. "Hi, Ethan. Is everything OK? You look stressed."

"I'm good," he said. "About tonight, it's all set up."

"I should be there," she said. "But there's the club meeting, and I don't know what I could do anyway."

"No, it's better this way. Business as usual. We don't want to tip off Morrigan, who's working tonight, or Cherney either, for that matter. Anyway, Captain Armen is staking them out. I feel pretty safe with him on watch. I'll see you after your meeting?"

"Yes," she said, "I'd like that." He started to leave when she took his hand. "Ethan, be careful."

***

At four thirty, he went down to his basement shop and stored away his cleaning supplies.

He put on a different shirt, a dress shirt that he had brought that morning, and checked himself in the bathroom mirror. He still looked more like a custodian than a high-dollar agent. But then, he figured Hanover had enough sophistication for them both.

At fifteen minutes to five, he went out the back way to his car, where he sat by himself for a moment to gather his nerve for what lay ahead. Pretending to be someone he was not in such a high-stakes game as this left him feeling vulnerable.

He parked in the hotel garage, made his way to the lobby, and took the elevator up to Hanover's room. The hallway, smelling of ammonia and soap, was still damp from mopping. The cleaning crew must have left for the day. He wondered when he'd started noticing such things. He knocked on Hanover's door and waited.

When there was no answer, he knocked again. There was no sound, save for a distant horn honking. His stomach tightened at the silence. He checked his watch. It was five thirty on the money. He stepped back and looked down the hallway. The sunset lit the distant window in orange.

He put his face close to the door. "Mr. Hanover?" he said, a bit more urgently. "It's me, Ethan. Are you ready?"

His resolve slipped a little in the silence, a brief moment in which he panicked at the lack of a response from inside. Had Hanover skipped town at the last minute, or had he worked a deal on the side with Cherney? Maybe he'd just lost his nerve and decided to call the whole thing a wash. Or maybe he'd been discovered and was floating under the park lake pier.

He knocked again, louder this time. A fluorescent light flickered overhead. He tried the doorknob, and the door opened.

"Mr. Hanover, are you in there?" he asked. "We're running out of time."

Had he misunderstood the time? Was he waiting downstairs in the lobby? Ethan had been clear that they were to go together. He checked his watch again and stepped in.

The room was dark and silent. The bed was made, and a pair of house shoes was parked next to the nightstand. A tray from room service was on the stand but appeared to be untouched.

"Mr. Hanover?" he said again. "It's me, Ethan Poser. Are you ready?"

The bathroom door was ajar, but no glow came from inside. He pushed the door open and reached his hand inside to turn on the light. In the sudden glare, he leaned against the doorjamb, his stomach knotting at the sight before him.

Jason Hanover lay half naked on the floor. One arm was curled under him; the other reached out toward the door. Blood trickled from the corner of his mouth and gathered beneath his cheek. His face was pale and opaque, like candle wax, and his eyes were open. There was the slightest bloat about him, and the sweet smell of death lingered in the closeness of the bathroom. Ethan struggled to regain his composure.

"Damn you, Hanover," he said in a whisper. "Couldn't you have waited? What am I to do now?"

He looked at his watch. He would be late to the meeting, and what would Cherney think if he showed up alone? What would he think if he didn't show up at all?

He dialed Captain Armen's cell phone. It rang, finally kicking over to voicemail. There wasn't time for this. He had to make a decision—go, or not go? He looked back into the bathroom, then turned for the door. Jason Hanover or no Jason Hanover, he couldn't miss that meeting with Cherney. He'd figure out what to tell him on his way there.

Chapter 40

Anna put the coffee on and arranged the chairs in the Genealogy Room. Imani was to present her book tonight, and Anna wanted everything to be ready. Diego arrived early, as was his way, and helped Anna get things in order. He had grown quiet and subdued over the weeks, and she wondered if things were getting difficult for him. Finding a job with limited English skills would be a struggle at best, and he'd taken to spending almost all of his waking hours at the library.

"Is Ethan going to join the club soon?" he asked. "Maybe the books are too big?"

She glanced up at the clock. Ethan and Hanover should be at the bookstore that very minute. She cleared her throat. "I don't think that's it. He's been quite busy lately." To change the subject, she asked, "Have you read Imani's selection yet, Diego?"

"Oh, sure," he said. "A very good book. I think I must be afraid to be invisible."

She paused. "Are you OK, Diego? You seem a little down."

He set the last chair at the end of the table. "I am OK, Anna, but it is very hard for finding jobs in America if your English is not so good."

"Diego, did you know that the library has a program for teaching English as a second language? Maybe you should think about signing up."

"Maybe it cost a lot of money?" he said.

"Well, there is tuition and books."

"I will think about taking such a program soon," he said.

The other members began to drift in: Doris Gill with her spangle earrings, Van Number, his bald pate shining under the lights, and Imani Bell, who had dressed for the occasion, her hair quaffed, a large pearl necklace covering her ample breasts. She took up her place near the front and began reviewing her notes for the session.

Anna had heard nothing from Mia Layla and Dakota Chance since their arrest by Captain Armen. It was too bad, really. Mia had demonstrated a quick understanding of the ideas that arose during the book discussions, although Dakota, with his pitch-black hair and chiseled looks, struggled to participate. She suspected that Mia had been trapped in the relationship.

All in all, the group had bonded over the weeks of reading and discussing their books. They were diverse in age, race, and experiences but had drawn together under the guise of Book Club Central to ponder the commonality of their own smaller worlds. At first Anna had resisted the assignment, another task added to her already busy schedule, but she'd come to care about each of the members and what they brought to the group.

Anna went to the podium. "May I have your attention." She waited as they assumed their places. "As you know, Imani is presenting her selection tonight. We have all read the book, and I'm sure there are many questions. Imani, would you come up now, please?"

Imani gathered up her things and walked to the front. The podium was high for her, but she was undaunted, looking out over the group with her quick, black eyes.

"Tonight," she said, "I will be discussing *The Invisible Man,* written by Ralph Ellison. I want you to keep these facts in mind as we discuss this book. Ralph Ellison, a Black man, wrote this book in 1947. Not only did he write it but he also won the National Book Award for it. Do you have any idea how special a book had to be to garner such recognition for a man of color in 1947?

"But I'm assuming, if you read this book, you have appreciation for not only its literary merit but its vision. Everything that Ralph Ellison struggled with in 1947—the lack of available education, the debilitating effects of discrimination, the absence of hope—is as true today as it was then.

"We are still afraid to dream, and we still think and talk in terms of race. It's the first point and the last of every issue. Ellison says that *that,* in itself, endangers the dream, and that any act that endangers the dream is treason. It's not so much about wealth, or lack of it, as it is about the loss of dignity. It's about humiliation and shame. Ellison says that we Black people are judged even by what we eat. Yams, sweet potatoes, melons, are used to define us and embarrass us. How absurd to be judged by the fare that was afforded."

Doris Gill held up her hand. "What does he mean by the *invisible* man? Isn't being Black, the most visible thing, the biggest issue?"

Imani stepped from behind the podium so that all could see her. "It's not so much the color of my skin," she said, holding out her arms for them to see. "It's the fact that when the white world looks at me, they don't see me as a mother, a student, an intelligence. They don't see those things, because I exist first and only as the one thing they do not want to see. I'm like that old piece of furniture you have, the one you've had for ages, the one you no longer see as valuable, or pretty, or special. It's there, useful at times, and where it has always been, so you don't see it. It has become unseen."

"But how does a person *make* someone see them?" Doris asked.

Imani looked around the room. She had grown taller, bigger in her presence, in the last few moments. "The only one who can change *what* they see is the one who is looking," she said. "When you see me for the first time for who I am, it is through your eyes, not mine.

"Even our struggle to be seen has not changed: the protest, the never-ending struggle for equality. We are killed today as we were in 1947. Like Ellison said of Brother Tarp, who had a limp, though his leg was healthy. It was caused from dragging a chain around for years.

The chain was still there, though no one could see it, and he couldn't know that it was gone."

"But protest could become violent, then and now," Van said. "What about that?"

Imani turned to Van. "Like Ellison said, 'sometimes the difference between individual and organized indignation is the difference between criminal and political action.' He also said, 'We must strive to reach the people through intelligence.' That is why I am here, and I think it's the reason you are here as well."

Chapter 41

Ethan stood in front of the bookstore. He rolled his shoulders against the tension and took a deep breath. He practiced what he would say. Hanover couldn't make it. He was a busy man, last-minute business, something unexpected that had to be dealt with in a timely manner. He sent his apologies, and they would reschedule the meeting as soon as possible.

Ethan opened the door, and the bell jingled his arrival. The girl at the desk lifted her gaze from the book she was reading. "May I help you?"

"I've a meeting with Mr. Cherney," he said.

She picked up the phone, watching him as she talked. "You may go on back. He's expecting you."

Ethan worked his way through the shelves, the smell of books, the passing of memories. Cherney was waiting at the door of the rare books room.

"Mr. Bosley," he said. "Where is your client?"

Ethan stepped in. "He had a last-minute business emergency and asked me to relay his apologies."

"A business emergency?"

"Yes, it was necessary that he deal with it right away. He plans to reschedule as soon as possible."

"I see," he said. "That's unfortunate, since we have brought the book here today for him to examine. You do think that he's still interested in the book?"

"He's very sorry, Mr. Cherney, and he's absolutely still interested."

"Then I suppose there is no need to proceed now?"

"Well, since you have the book, and I'm here, perhaps I could take a look?"

"A book such as this should not be handled any more than is necessary. It's quite fragile."

"I'll be careful," Ethan said.

"Well, I suppose," he said, with an obvious anticipation of his own, as if he needed an excuse to see the book again himself. "Please put on the gloves, Mr. Poser, and do turn the pages carefully."

When Cherney returned, he gingerly laid the book down in front of Ethan, who opened it to the title page.

"This is the translation?" he asked, trying to remember exactly what Hanover had told him about the book.

"That's correct, Benjamin Motte, translator. London. It's paneled calf, as you can see."

"Beautiful," Ethan said.

"If you are authorized to make an offer, we'd be happy to entertain it," Cherney said.

"At these prices, my client prefers to negotiate his own terms. I'm sure you can appreciate that."

The girl from the front desk knocked on the window. Cherney dropped his glasses around his neck.

"Excuse me for a moment," he said, stepping out.

The girl, animated, was saying something to Cherney. He looked in at Ethan, then said something back to her.

When he returned, he was quiet, sullen. He closed the book and said, "I've someone coming in, Mr. Bosley, if there is nothing else."

"It's a fine copy," Ethan said. "I'm sure my client will be rescheduling."

"Yes, I'm sure. Good day to you."

***

Ethan had pulled to a stop at the intersection on Main when Captain Armen drove up alongside and motioned for him to pull over. Ethan took the next turn and pulled into a parking lot, the captain parking next to him. Captain Armen walked toward Ethan's car. The weapon hanging from his belt magnified an already intimidating figure.

Ethan rolled down his window, and Armen leaned in. "When Cherney went for the book, we were able to follow him to the warehouse," he said. "We are waiting on a warrant now."

"That's great," Ethan said.

"So how did the meeting go?"

"Captain Armen," Ethan said, "we need to talk."

***

Ethan followed the captain back to the Reston Hotel, where they got a pass key, then took the elevator up. When they stepped into the hallway, Armen turned to him.

"Was Cherney suspicious about Hanover's absence?"

"Cherney is a cold fish, Captain. It's hard to know. I told him my client had a last-minute business emergency. He showed me the *Principia*. I told him we'd get back to him. He wasn't all that pleased."

Outside the door of Hanover's room, Armen paused. "Are you sure he's dead?"

"I've not seen a lot of dead bodies before, Captain, but I'm pretty sure on this one."

The room was dark, save for the light bleeding from the half-open bathroom door. Armen pulled his weapon, holding it against his thigh as he eased the door back. And there was Hanover's body, still on the floor. Armen holstered his weapon and knelt down for a closer look.

"He's been dead a while," he said. "Hours at the least. But I don't see any wounds."

"He was a sick man, Captain. Maybe it caught up with him."

"I'll have to call homicide in. There will be an investigation, an autopsy. This is great timing."

In the bedroom, Armen phoned the homicide division and explained the situation, that a search warrant was in progress and that he needed to move on it.

In the elevator, on the way back down to the lobby, he turned to Ethan. "We watched the bookstore for half a day. When Cherney came out, we tailed him to a warehouse on Washington Street. We can't enter without a warrant. In the meantime, it's business as usual for you. Stay out of Morrigan's way, and don't stir anything up until we have this situated."

In the parking garage, they arrived at Ethan's parked car. Ethan made to unlock it, then stopped, pausing thoughtfully.

"What?" Captain Armen said.

"Hanover was just helping, Captain."

"Yeah, I know," he said, turning away toward his vehicle.

Chapter 42

Ethan pulled out onto the highway. Anna and Book Club Central should still be at the library. Imani was to give her talk tonight, and Dr. Morrigan was staying late for a board meeting. It would give him a chance to make sure the library was secured. There had been a lot of activity going on in the parking lot, and then with the Special Collections thing. And just maybe he would catch Anna when she'd finished with the club. They needed to talk, or at least he did.

He entered through the back door of the library to find that all the main lights were off in the library proper. Morrigan's office was still lit, but no one was around. He could hear Anna and the other club members talking in the Genealogy Room. The group laughed, followed by light clapping.

He slipped past the Genealogy Room on his way to the basement. His shop was dark, save for the evening light coming from the high, narrow window of the basement. He could hear the distant sounds of the book club through the heating vents overhead.

He searched for his desk light—then suddenly realized he was not alone. Who was there in the darkness he didn't know, but there was no mistaking the cold muzzle of the revolver pressed against the back of his neck.

Dr. Bates Morrigan moved to the other side of Ethan's desk and sat down in the chair. The light from the window reflected in the thick lenses of his glasses, small rainbows that lit and faded when he moved. His weapon was leveled at Ethan.

"What's this about?" Ethan asked, his voice breaking.

"Got a call from a friend of mine today," he said. "A Mr. Baden Cherney. You might have heard of him. Apparently, Mr. Cherney has been mistaking you for someone with the name of Ross Bosley, until today, that is, when his clerk correctly identified you as Ethan Poser. He wondered if I knew the name. He says you've been presenting yourself as an agent for the purchase of some very valuable merchandise."

Ethan's mouth turned to cotton. "Morrigan,

I know what you've been up to, how you've been stealing from the collection and fencing it through Hathaway's."

"That so?" he said. "Unfortunate timing, Mr. Poser. You see, the foundation board has scheduled an appraisal of the collection. I was thinking it might be a good time for me to go on vacation. Now you've spoiled it."

"There's a small matter of murder here too," Ethan said.

Morrigan puffed air through his lips and leaned back in the chair. "Belowe? That little man was a blackmailer, snooping around, looking for an opportunity to con someone."

"So you took him for a swim in the park lake?"

"Belowe should have minded his own business, like you, Poser. I've handled the most important and rarest books anywhere in the world. I have years of experience dealing with high-end collectors. I'm an expert in areas most people can't fathom, a valuable asset to this library, and someone who has built a world-class collection. And then Belowe comes along, a custodian, a con, thinking he's going to blackmail me. And now you. I don't think so, Poser. Not a chance."

"Look what you've done to the collection," Ethan said. "You were the guardian, the caretaker. Its existence depended on you, and you've diminished it for money."

Morrigan's breath quickened, whether from regret or anger Ethan couldn't know. What he did know was that Morrigan had already killed once.

"Do you know what I earn as director of this place, Poser? And that collection is worth millions. It wouldn't exist without me. What I've taken, I've earned."

"What about the donors, Morrigan? What about those who spent their lives and fortunes putting their collections together? They trusted you with their care. Didn't you owe them something?"

"Collectors," he said, looking off. "You think they care about mankind, or knowledge, or have some high-minded notion of preserving the past for humanity? I've dealt with them my whole life, compulsive and driven as they are. They only want the first, or the most, or the rarest, trade rats looking for the next shiny object. What do I owe them?"

Laughter from Book Club Central drifted down through the vents, miniature and distant, like voices from a vintage phonograph.

"Maybe they're just people who love history, Morrigan, love books and knowledge, and want to preserve them for posterity."

"And what would you know, a custodian, sweeping floors and cleaning up after people?" He rose from the desk chair. "Stand up, Poser."

Ethan stood, his legs weak under him. If he left the library with Morrigan, there would be no reprieve.

"Where are we going?" he asked.

Morrigan pointed the revolver toward the stairs. "A little walk," he said.

They made their way up the basement steps, Ethan in the lead, Morrigan behind with his weapon. Ethan could hear Morrigan breathing, labored and shallow in the closeness of the stairwell. He figured Morrigan was not a man practiced with a weapon. He was a scholar, not a warrior, but he did have the revolver, and it was pointed at Ethan's back.

They eased past the Genealogy Room, the door ajar, a crack of light in the darkness. Ethan could see Imani at the podium. Diego was on the front row. Next to him was Doris Gill. Van Number's foot was bouncing, his arms folded. Imani gathered up her notes, and the group clapped.

Ethan caught a quick glance of Anna as she was walking to the front of the room. He hoped he was to see her again, to tell her how much he admired her.

"Out the front," Morrigan said in a whisper. "And keep it quiet."

Rows of books stood like soldiers, like guards at attention. Ethan could see the Victorian doors ahead, their windows tinted with the sunset. Uncertainty awaited beyond them. If he was to act, it had to be soon.

They were nearly to the door. Laughter drifted from the distance. Ahead was the security gate, an electronic contraption designed to discourage book theft by the public.

"Go," Morrigan said.

In that final second, Ethan swept up a book from the shelf and stepped through the security gate. The alarm lifted into the high reaches of the rotunda, a singular and relentless pulse that sent shock waves into Ethan's core.

Morrigan struck him a blow from behind. The room went askew, lights bursting in his eyes, and he staggered into the shelves. Morrigan swung him around, knocking books onto the floor, and shoved him back the way they had come.

They climbed the stairs with Morrigan pushing and cursing from behind him, the security monitor throbbing. Somewhere below them, voices rose up, anxious and intense. Blood, smelling of iron, coursed down Ethan's head, and the world whirled about him.

He could hear Morrigan behind, jamming and grunting his way upward. Then Ethan realized that they had come to the mezzanine. Its stillness and calm and its cavernous resonance surrounded them.

Morrigan worked at the Special Collections door, fumbling the key in the lock, all the while watching Ethan with an unerring eye. He shoved the door open and motioned Ethan in. Locking the door behind him, he spun around, striking Ethan with a vicious blow in the face.

Ethan crumpled to the floor, the crack of his teeth like pebbles in his mouth. He hung his head between his arms, pink drooling onto the floor. He struggled to stand, but the floor shifted beneath him.

What was Morrigan's plan, why here on third? It didn't make sense. Perhaps there was an alternate way out, or perhaps it was instinct, a rat running to its hole. Morrigan grabbed him by the hair and dragged him backward through the files, back to where the ancient tomes lay silent in crypts of vellum and calf. Perhaps it was here among the forebears that he was most in charge, most certain of his deeds. But all about him were the remnants of his crime, of his destruction and wanton disregard for all that had come before.

Like toads they huddled in the darkness, listening to the sounds of footsteps and the clamor of voices at the door. Morrigan's pistol rested on Ethan's neck, a cold reminder of its lethality.

"No one gets into Special Collections," he said under his breath. "I have the key."

But Morrigan was in error, this Ethan knew, because twice he and Anna had breached the shrine themselves. It was not impenetrable, as Morrigan thought, not so long as Anna had access to the locked file cabinet.

Suddenly, like a small, bright explosion, the door burst open, letting out a clatter of voices and instructions and scutterings about. Morrigan's breath rushed away in surprise. Stunned by the invasion of Book Club Central, he stood in disbelief that the sanctum had been violated.

It was an opportunity presented, and one Ethan took, swinging blindly to knock away

Morrigan's weapon, which skidded off into the row of file cabinets that perched against the back wall. He waited for the pain, his wrist broken from the blow, and when it came, he cried out in agony.

Morrigan looked around, frantic for his weapon. Not finding it, he headed down the aisle, only to see Book Club Central gathered there.

"I've caught a book thief," Morrigan said, yelling. "Poser, the custodian. He was stealing from the collection and tried to escape through the front door."

Anna stepped forward. "I'm afraid not, Dr. Morrigan. It's you who is the thief, you and Baden Cherney of Hathaway's bookstore. It's you who is the murderer of Clarence Belowe. We have the proof, you see. Captain Armen is searching your warehouse at this very moment."

Morrigan turned and ran back past Ethan in an attempt to escape up the adjoining aisle, but Diego had it blocked. Anna, Imani Bell, and Van Number scrambled past Ethan. Seeing Diego, Morrigan whirled around to retreat once again but came face-to-face with Book Club Central. By then, Doris Gill, her bad knee having slowed her down, joined the pack. She held her purse over her shoulder, a battle-axe at the ready. Like wolves they waited for the right moment to attack.

By then, Diego, a deft and fearless opponent, had reached Morrigan. Diego locked his arm about Morrigan's neck. They struggled into the stacks, Diego's relentless hold taking its toll on Morrigan's strength. But Morrigan was angry, determined, and, most of all, frightened.

The others joined in to subdue him, and a struggle ensued. Anna suffered a blow to her nose, Imani to her cheek. Van, overweight and out of shape, gasped for breath as he tried to pin Morrigan's arms. Diego, in an attempt to pull Morrigan to the floor, fell backward into the bookshelves, which began a slow but inevitable topple into the aisle.

The others pounced on Morrigan, holding him down. The smell of dust and antiquity filled the room and settled over them. Anna, her hair covered in dust, sat on the floor. Blood dripped from her nose and into a corner of her mouth. Imani, her eye bruised and swollen, came to Ethan's aid, while Diego and Van worked to secure Morrigan's wrists with a roll of duct tape they found in the supply room. In the distance, the *beep-beep* of the security alarm persisted in its mission to warn of a stolen book.

Ethan pulled himself to Anna's side and took her hand. "Thanks for the rescue," he said.

A light shone in Anna's eyes. "We came to stop a book thief," she said, "and I guess we did."

Doris Gill went back to the office to call Captain Armen, while the others gathered around, Book Club Central all, so different one from the other, so alike in valor and spirit.

***

Captain Armen and a deputy soon arrived. They cuffed Morrigan, and the deputy took him away for processing. Book Club Central waited in the Genealogy Room for the captain to finish up.

When he came in, he said, "This case is going to take some time. We don't have a clear fix yet on the damage that's been done. Anna, could you make arrangements for a complete inventory check? Meanwhile, we will be taking statements from each of you about what took place here this evening.

"That said, I'd like to thank each of you

for not letting this man get away. You're the darndest book club I've come across lately. If I'd known how brave reading books could make a fella, I'd have taken it up myself a long time ago.

"Ethan and Anna, we will be waiting on the autopsy results on Jason Hanover. Don't leave town until we get that resolved."

Ethan said, "What about Baden Cherney, Captain?"

"I've always said I didn't believe much in coincidences, but just as me and the deputy drove up on that warehouse, guess who was already there? That's right, Baden Cherney. Turns out that warehouse is chock full of stolen books. Cherney was right happy to see us, as you can imagine."

"And what about the *Principia*?" Anna asked.

"Cherney had it with him. I admit to not being impressed by the looks of that old book."

"Where is it now?" Anna asked.

"In the trunk of my car."

"The *Principia* is in your car trunk?" Anna said.

"Last I checked."

"But what if someone steals it?"

The captain paused and looked around the room. "Well, we got Book Club Central here to catch 'em up if they do, don't we?"

Chapter 43

Two weeks after Morrigan was arrested, Ethan finally had a chance to sleep in. He'd been working double time keeping the library clean, while helping Anna conduct a complete inventory of Special Collections. She'd been asked by the board to temporarily take over Morrigan's position, while holding down her own workload as well. Both the captain and the foundation were anxious to know about the damage that had incurred.

They had worked day and night since to finish the assessment. For Ethan, although the hours had been long, they hadn't been entirely unpleasant. Not only did he enjoy spending time with Anna but his daily plunge into the rare book world had been gratifying. There were moments when he'd been swept up into other worlds and times that he'd had no idea existed.

The loss to Special Collections was staggering—millions of dollars of the rarest and most valuable books were missing. Many of those had been stolen over a twenty-five-year span. The thefts had been so slow and methodical that no one had detected them. Without oversight, Morrigan had simply walked out the front door of the library and taken them down the street to Hathaway's Used and Rare Books, where they were sold and disbursed to collectors and even to institutions worldwide. Now, years later, they would be nearly impossible to track down. Both Morrigan and Cherney had been criminally charged and awaited trial, but their sentences were of little consolation given the crippling losses to Special Collections.

The experience had in many ways reinforced what Ethan already knew: his tenure as a custodian was coming to an end. It had served its purpose, but it was not what he wanted or needed for his life's work. At some point, it would fail him. He wanted challenge and stimulation and a reason to go on.

And so, without saying anything to anyone, he had initiated a job search. It was not without misgivings, because he had become fond of Anna. She had an intensity and joy about her that was engaging, the way she spiked her arms on her waist, rolled her eyes, and smiled. He thought that she cared for him, but he'd thought that once before, about another woman in his life. It was not a mistake he should make again.

***

Ethan finished his morning coffee and headed out to work, taking his usual trek through the park. He'd gotten as far as the pier where Belowe had met his end when he spotted the little dog near the swing set. The dog tipped his head and watched Ethan for a moment before slinking away into the trees.

Ethan wondered at what he must have endured, alone, lost, and hungry, as he clearly was. By the looks of him, he could not have been eating much, perhaps scraps left over from the occasional picnic. Although he'd managed to escape the dog catcher, his odds were not good. Ethan didn't care to think of what would happen to him in the city pound.

When Ethan arrived at work, Anna, wearing a black pant suit with a sterling buckle, was waiting. She smiled at him, her eyes the color of olives.

"Wow," he said. "You look nice. What's going on?"

"I've been promoted to director of the library, Ethan. I can't believe this has happened. I'm so excited."

"That's wonderful, Anna. You deserve it, and you will make a terrific director."

"Oh, thank you," she said. "It's something I've always wanted. Ethan, would you ask Diego to come to the office?"

"Ah, sure. Now?"

"Yes, please. Oh, and will you be around at lunch? I'll be gone for a couple hours this morning, but I'd like to talk to you before you go home."

"Bologna sandwich in the basement," he said. "I only brought one, but you can have Diego's banana."

"I'll see you later, then," she said.

He found Diego snoozing behind a magazine. "Anna wants to see you. I think you might be in serious trouble."

Diego rubbed his eyes. "I have done nothing wrong. I read the news magazines so that I will be a best citizen like you."

"Right," Ethan said. "Try reading with your eyes open. That's the way we do it in America. Well, a few of us do, anyway."

***

He'd eaten his lunch and was about to go back to work when Anna came down the stairs.

"Can you talk now, Ethan?"

"Of course," he said, smiling. "You're the boss, aren't you? Sit down." He motioned to the desk chair.

Anna sat down and rested her purse on his desk. "I've just left my first official board meeting as director of the library, and I have some information to share."

"With me?"

"Yes, in fact, it concerns you."

"Oh?"

"You see, since I've taken the library director's position, we find ourselves short of an associate librarian."

"I'm sure you'll fill the position soon."

"Yes, well, the board asked me if I could recommend someone." She leaned forward on his desk, her hands together, and slipped her thumbs under her chin. Her olive eyes locked on his. "I've recommended you for the position, Ethan."

Ethan lowered his head and looked at her.

"That's flattering, Anna, but I'm the custodian, remember?"

"Working as a custodian does not necessarily *make* you a custodian, Ethan. You have an education and a good mind, and you have a passion for these books. I have seen it."

"But what about the custodial job?"

"The board also asked my recommendation for that position."

"And?"

"Diego has agreed to take it."

"But I know nothing about being a librarian, Anna."

"You would have to become certified at some point as an archivist, but that can be accomplished while you are working."

"What would all this entail?"

"The usual duties of maintaining and updating stock. Meeting the needs of our patrons will be part of the job too, but I would be here to assist, of course." She turned in the chair for a moment before turning back. "But there is more involved here than the usual library duties, Ethan. You see, the board wants Special Collections rebuilt to its past glory. The first step will be to locate and retrieve the most valuable of the books that remain missing. A large part of your duties would be to assist in tracking those down and bringing them home."

"But the books could be anywhere. How can they be located? What chance of getting them back, even if they're found?"

"I didn't say it would be easy. Rare book collectors are often wealthy and powerful people. They know how to get what they want and are willing to pay the price. You need to understand that there could be personal risk involved."

"But why me for the position? I'm hardly an expert in the rare book world."

"The board considered this at length. They've decided that you have the one thing that's mandatory for success."

"What would that be?"

"You are willing to learn."

Ethan stood. He wasn't at all certain that he was capable of such an assignment, or that he'd done anything other than gotten caught up in unusual circumstances; besides, he'd already made the decision that it was time to move on.

"I'm not sure, Anna."

"I understand. You need some time to think it over?"

"Yes, I need to think this through."

"There is one other thing I'd like you to know."

"And what's that?"

"I didn't make this recommendation lightly, and this is not about my personal feelings. This job will require resolve and intelligence. You have both. Let me know when you know. There's work to be done."

***

Ethan walked into the evening. The remnants of the sun draped the horizon like liquid gold. It had been a hell of a day, a day both gratifying and stressful. Anna had taken one step more than was expected of her. That's how he saw it, or maybe it was how he wanted to see it.

His own feelings were confused as well. He couldn't deny that he was drawn to her as much as he'd ever been to anyone. But he'd been there before, and it had nearly broken him. Though Anna had made it clear that her decision was strictly business, he wasn't sure he could make the same claim. And then, of course, there was the job itself, one for which he was unprepared, and an assignment that might well exceed his skills.

He entered the park in the last of the sunset. The smell of the lake and the sorrowful coo of a mourning dove somewhere beyond the swings edged into his consciousness. The old pier stretched off into the water. He walked out to its end and could hear the soft slapping of the waves against the pillars. The image of Clarence Belowe's body floating in the dark water below came to him, and he turned back for shore.

As he stepped off the pier, he realized that the little dog was watching him nervously from the trees beyond the swings. Even at that distance, he could see that he was faring poorly. He was gaunt and weary. Not wanting to frighten him away, Ethan sat down at the end of the pier and whistled softly for him to come. But he retreated a little further, fearful, stopping just short of the tree line.

Ethan stood to go when he spotted a dog collar half buried in the mud. He washed its mud-caked tag clean in the lake water—"Scooter," a phone number, and the name of Clarence Belowe, 415 Beasley St., Middleton, PA.

He called out the dog's name. "Scooter!" The little dog lifted his head, and Ethan called once more. Scooter moved forward, cautiously at first, then at full trot, toward Ethan.

Ethan held out his hands. "Come here, Scooter," he said.

And he did, his feet bouncing. Ethan sat back down and pulled him in. Scooter trembled with uncertainty as he leaned into him. Ethan could feel his ribs beneath his shaggy coat.

"Scooter," he said, "I've been asked by a pretty lady to go on an exciting journey to hunt for lost treasure and serve up justice when it's called for. She tells me that it might be a bit dangerous here and there but that it will be worth the risk. She says I have a lot to learn but that I'm capable. What do you think?"

Puzzled, Scooter cocked his head and looked up at him. Ethan stroked his back. "Not sure, huh? You know you have an interest in serving up justice yourself, don't you? What if I were to invite you to come along as my partner? We'd make a hell of a team." Scooter rose up on his back feet, placed his front paws on Ethan's chest, and looked him straight in the eyes. His tail spun like an electric fan. "I think so too," Ethan said. "Come on, partner. Let's go home."

Author's Note

Although *A Rare Obsession* and its characters are fictional, the idea to write the book was inspired by an actual theft of rare books from the Carnegie Library in Pittsburgh, Pennsylvania, where more than $8.1 million worth of rare books were stolen over a quarter century and sold through a nearby rare book store.

A special thank-you to my editor, Holly Monteith. Her skills as an editor are matched only by her keen intellect and dedication to the craft. *A Rare Obsession* has benefited from her work.

And thanks as always to my wife, Nancy, who has encouraged and sustained me for more than six decades of marriage.

I also thank the librarians and book club members of the world for their contributions to literature. Their love of books helps keep our stories alive.

Dr. Sheldon Russell, Professor Emeritus, is the author of fifteen books, including his award-winning historical fiction and his popular Hook Runyon mystery series. His books have garnered three Oklahoma Book Awards for Fiction, the Langum Prize for Historical Literature, and the Spur Award for Best Historical Western from the Western Writers of America. His books have earned starred reviews from both *Booklist* and *Publishers Weekly*. Russell is a graduate of Northwestern Oklahoma State University and Oklahoma State University. He currently lives on the family ranch in the beautiful Gloss Mountains of northwestern Oklahoma.

Loved It?

Join the Reader's Nook
to enjoy exclusive early access to new releases, special promotions, and news about forthcoming books from Cennan Books and Cynren Press.

www.ingramcontent.com/pod-product-compliance
Lightning Source LLC
Chambersburg PA
CBHW052354131025
33985CB00030B/449